I0659158

One More Score
A Mystic Realms Novella

By
Anton Kukal

Mystic Realms, Ltd
2022

One More Score
A Mystic Realms Novella

Published by Mystic Realms, Ltd.

This is a work of fiction. Names, characters, businesses, places, events, and incidents are either the products of the author's imagination or used in a fictitious manner. Any resemblance to actual persons, living or dead, or actual events is purely coincidental.

Mystic Realms, Ltd.
PO Box 666
Millville, NJ 08332

Mystic Realms® is a registered trademark of Mystic Realms, Ltd.

ISBN: 978-1-932005-30-1 print
ISBN: 978-1-932005-31-8 mobi

Printed in the United States of America

Dedication

For my wife, Bobbi, who

has always encouraged me to pursue my dreams,

and for my children,

Alexandra, Anthony, and Emily

Other Books By
ANTON KUKAL

Aggie-9

Death Wagon

Lieutenant Steel

The Robot MAIM

TRUDY

Contents

Chapter One

Franky yee-hawed with wild glee as he jerked the steering wheel of our stolen cargo van to the right, lifting the left tires a few inches off the ground.

"Slow down," I said.

Instead of slowing, Franky accelerated. "I got this, old man."

The twenty-year-old kid revved the van's engine, flung the steering wheel back to the left, slammed on the brakes, and fishtailed for thirty feet. His resumé included running moonshine for his uncle and driving tanks for the army, so I hired him as a driver. My mistake. I clung to the arm rests of my seat with a white-knuckled grip, and started to worry.

The van's engine revved even louder as he approached the red light, then the brakes squealed. Franky veered hard to the right as he crossed the intersection, narrowly missing two elderly pedestrians crossing the street. Panicked, they dropped their shopping bags. Canned goods and soda bottles rolled through the crosswalk. The old man shook his cane in anger as the woman bent to collect their groceries before the light changed.

I looked out the van's side window. Two orb-shaped hover cameras from the local news agency followed us, their jet propulsion systems easily keeping pace with our van. They had been with us since we left the highway. Probably attracted by Franky's erratic driving.

The kid swerved to avoid the backed-up traffic that was stopped at the next intersection. The right tire bounced over the curb, and our van crashed through two sidewalk tables filled with comic book memorabilia, mostly action-figures and poster tubes. The little plastic dolls flew into the air, tiny arms and legs whirling, a kaleidoscope of spinning color. I recognized Vortex, WiggleChins, Sludge, DoctorHelix, and a few others as the figures bounced off our windshield. The vendors backed away shaking their fists as our van sped passed.

"That's going to look great on video," Franky announced.

Did the kid purposely hit those tables? Was he trying to show off for the news cameras?

"Get back on the street," I told him.

Franky bounced off the sidewalk into the intersection, narrowly missing a trash can. He accelerated fast, honking at the cross traffic, as he turned left and increased our speed to almost double the limit. Racing down the street, he swerved around vehicles and ran two more red lights.

"You're going to miss the bank!" I warned, pointing at the building coming up on the right.

"I got this, old man."

Franky slammed on the brake pedal, jerked the steering wheel, and the cargo van drifted sideways, tires screeching, into the no parking zone in front of the First National Bank building.

"How was that?" Franky asked Joe who was seated in the passenger's seat.

Joe, my good friend and boss of more than forty years, looked a little pale. He released his grip and shook out his stiff fingers. "Maybe a little slower next time."

"Boss," Franky said, "you gotta make an entrance. You're a supervillain. You need shock and awe, flash and flare. That's what people want these days."

Joe pulled on his mask and became the comic book legend, SafeCracker, who had the power to control mechanical devices. He could open any lock and make machines do his bidding.

SafeCracker turned to me. "Are you ready?"

"Sure, boss." I pulled my black mask down over my face.

My name is Gene. I'm SafeCracker's head henchman. I'm more than a minion. I have responsibilities. On the job, I run the crew. SafeCracker gives the orders, and I make sure the thugs follow them. Off the job, I keep the books, pay the bills, and do practically everything so SafeCracker can focus on being a supervillain. He's the big name, and I'm the guy that keeps his name big.

I took a deep breath, more out of habit than nerves. Over the past forty years, Joe and I have perfected the art of bank robbery. We just follow the plan, step by step, handling each crisis as it arises, until we get away. We've robbed so many banks together I could probably steal the money with my eyes closed. I'd consider trying, but honestly, I am getting too old to fool around. Just go in, secure the room, crack the vault, get the cash, and hope there are no major mishaps or screw-ups.

Joe looked past me to the back of the van. "Are the rest of you ready?"

Our hired muscle filled the two rear seats, five thugs and the girl, Carmella, who joined the team six months ago and acted tough enough to kick all their butts.

The guys were all the same. Big muscle-bound brutes who barely squeezed their bulk into their extra-large smoke-grey blouson jackets and baggy military pants, the kind with side pockets on the thigh. Black jackboots and body armor completed their minion image.

"I'm ready for anything," Carmella said.

She was sitting in the far back, between two thugs, looking

dangerous and beautiful. Her hair was that shocking shade of fire red. She styled it close-cropped on the left side of her head, but long and straight on the right. Her green eyes pinned me down with an 'I'll-shoot-you-dead-for-a-penny' stare that always gave me the chills.

I didn't like Carmella, not one bit. I know trouble when trouble hip-swings into the room for a job interview. I told Joe not to hire her, but Carmella batted those big eyelashes, flexed her ripped biceps, cracked her knuckles, and she got the job. She'd been trouble ever since, always piping up with ways to make things better, mostly ideas we tried years ago that didn't fit our style.

The thugs grabbed the empty money sacks and their fully automatic assault rifles. I hated those guns. Back in the old days, when we first started, a supervillain and his team didn't need guns. If the cops surrounded us and we couldn't fight our way out using our fists, we took our lumps. Nowadays, it is standard operating procedure for most minions to pull out their guns and turn the streets into a war zone.

I know the industry has changed. Hover cameras follow the action and the audience likes violence and loves explosions. These days it's all about ratings. I understand that, but I'm old school. I take pride in running a clean job. My missions are carefully planned to ensure no one gets hurt. Our thugs don't cause property damage. Sure, we don't make the headlines any more, but that's okay with us.

Joe and I agree there is no art to crime these days. It's all smash and grab. Just like Franky said, shock and awe, flash and flare. Call me a dinosaur, or a throwback, or whatever you want, but I liked the days when the audience appreciated a perfectly-planned, low-profile heist that didn't end with a gunfight and car chase.

I pulled open the side door and hopped out, feeling the impact of the ground up my shins and into my knees. My doctor told me I have arthritis and that I need to change my lifestyle. If he only knew....

Not letting my aching knees slow me down, I opened SafeCracker's door with a flourish for the circling hover cameras. They zipped in, focusing their lenses for a close-up.

I heard Joe's knees creak as he stepped out onto the street. His loose-fitting jumpsuit with black cape, boots, and wide belt screamed "classic supervillain." We both preferred the traditional design. The supervillains of this era had flashy costumes that showed too much of their chiseled, gym-baked bodies.

Besides the fact that no one wanted to see our stringy old man muscles, we preferred to be fully clothed when committing acts of crime. Don't think we were behind the times in suit technology, though. I'd updated SafeCracker's costume to the new super standards, just not the new super look.

The jumpsuit was layered Kevlar with hardened ceramic plates covering the torso, upper arms, and thighs, which added to his natural damage reduction. Heat sinks and cold dampeners gave Joe resistance to the two most popular super energies and gave the added benefit of keeping him warm in the winter and cool in the summer. I'd even widened the belt to help hide Joe's slight paunch around his midriff, but the costume remained "no frills effective," an icon of the age of classic villains, just the way we liked it.

The hover camera whirled around us. We might make the local evening news, but we would not be picked up by any of the big media outlets. Fast in. Fast out. We'd be gone before the police even showed up. Not much of a story and nothing that would interest an audience that feeds on firefights and fatalities.

I jerked a finger at the muscle. "Let's go."

The five thugs filed out, faceless in their black masks. Years ago, I got to know everyone's names. Our old gang was like a big extended family. Joe and I knew their wives and kids. We all took care of each other, living the glamorous life of a supervillain's team.

Those boom years were the best. Two decades of good times. We'd pull one or two jobs a season and just got richer and richer. SafeCracker comic books flew off the shelves, and we even had a few of our heists make the national news.

We had twenty great years, from the early 1980s to the turn of the century. In many ways, those times were better than anyone had a right to have. We had lots of laughs, daring escapes, and really big scores, but then around 2002 the team started breaking up. Marriages on the rocks, kids getting older, injuries, sick parents, basically all the standard excuses for getting out of the life.

Joe and I kept going. Robbing banks was all we knew and truth be told, we loved the comic scene. We put in another twenty years, working with hired muscle, sometimes teaming up with other villains, always trying to recapture those wonderful years before the old team broke up.

Now, I don't even know the names of our crew. We hire them from a thug temp agency and they come fully trained. All I need to do is give them the rundown of the mission and they execute my plan. It's much cheaper than trying to build a crew and saving money is important these days as we move towards retirement. The last couple of years have just been icing on the cake, a way to put a few more dollars into our IRAs and annuities.

Carmella flounced out of the van. The way she moved, all sinewy and slick, made me wonder if she had any bones at all. She invaded my personal space, like she always did, standing too close and seeming to think every man wanted her.

"I think we better tell him," she announced, looking at Joe.

"Tell who what?" I asked.

Carmella glanced in my direction. "Joe has something to tell you."

I hated the way she smiled, so cocksure, like she knew something I didn't. She hefted her assault rifle, cradling the stock in her arm so that the barrel pointed up to the sky and made her looked like some kind of action hero. Minions didn't take that kind of posture. I knew I'd have to speak with her after the job.

"It can wait," I said. "We're on the clock. Boss, you ready?"

Instead of taking the lead up the steps, Joe fidgeted by the van. He kept looking from Carmella to me, as if expecting something. Had something happened between them? No way. Forty years separated them. They had nothing in common, and she was a minion. Supervillains didn't have relationships with their minions. Those were the rules. Even if there was an attraction, professionals didn't act on it. Joe and I were always professional.

"I have to tell you something."

The look that passed between them chilled me to the bone. I know it's cliche, but I felt my heart clench up, and I got cold all over. The way their eyes met and held each other's gaze gave the impression that they had become a couple. No, it was impossible. Joe knew I couldn't stand Carmella. He knew I wanted to kick her from the team.

Carmella did spend most of her time with him. I took a deep breath and let it out real slow. I refused to jump to conclusions. Joe would not do that to us, not after all these years of working together as professionals. We had plans to retire together. The goal was to buy a beach house and enjoy the lives we always wanted.

"What's up, boss?" I asked.

"Listen, Gene," he said, haltingly. "I probably should have said something before now. Last night, after you went to bed, Carmella and I discussed a few changes to the plan."

"You changed the plan?" I gasped. "And you're telling me now?"

Somehow, Carmella had gotten to my friend. She'd spun his head and sucked him into one of her crazy ideas. I just knew she was smiling behind her mask. Chewing her bubblegum, and feeling like she had herself a victory. Did she? I wondered how much the plans had truly changed? Maybe he was just humoring her? Sometimes it was easier just to give in to the little things than to listen to her complain.

Joe spoke quickly, as if blurting out something he didn't want to say. "We're going to implement the changes. Carmella briefed the muscle last night. You just need to follow along."

My head was spinning. "Briefed the muscle? What changes?"

Carmella nodded her head, as if encouraging him to go on.

"Don't worry," Joe assured me, which only made me worry more. "The modifications won't affect much, and we'll get a bigger score."

Chapter Two

I glanced down at my watch. The second hand swept around. We were wasting precious moments. Banks heists had to be meticulously planned. A team needed to be in and out before the cops arrived, and certainly before the superheroes. Joe and I were much too old to be tangling with the new generation of supers who protected the city.

"Boss. We make the plans together," I said. "You and I. Forty years."

"It's mostly your plan," Carmella said. "I just made a few tweaks to get with the times."

"Tweaks?" I stammered. "Why?"

"I need more exposure," Joe said.

"More exposure?" I was confused.

"Shock and awe," Joe said, then added, "Flash and flare."

Now I understood what prompted Franky to act the way he did. He was hamming it up, trying to score points with Carmella by using her own words. Damn him. Damn her. How had this happened behind my back?

I was not happy about being kept out of the loop, but I guess a few small changes to the plan was a lot better than discovering Joe and Carmella had ... I couldn't even form the thought. I swallowed my pride and tried to be a team player. "Can you give me the run down of changes?"

"It's nothing too crazy." Joe gave my shoulder a friendly slug, like we did in the old days. "We're just looking to maximize our payout by hitting a few of the safe deposit boxes."

I shook my head. "The boxes are a waste of time."

"It's risk versus reward," Carmella said. "Sometimes people store expensive items in those boxes."

"And often it's just wills and useless paper." I looked at Joe. "We learned this lesson four decades ago."

"I'm going to pop a few open," Joe said with finality.

"Sure boss," I wasn't happy, but when the supervillain decides, the minion follows. Besides, arguing the point in front of the bank we were supposed to be robbing was ludicrous behavior.

"What else do I need to know?"

"We need a bit more action." Joe said. "The thugs are going to do some yelling. Threaten people. Maybe break something. You know, stuff to create excitement."

"Like running over sidewalk stands?" I asked.

He had the grace to look chagrined, but did not back down. "We need to raise the stakes. Your plans are just too smooth... Too perfect. I don't get noticed anymore."

"Scaring civilians and causing property damage is not our style."

"No body will get hurt," Joe said. "We just need a little turbulence to engage the younger crowd. They want action scenes. You know this business is all about getting fans."

"And you think wanton violence is the answer?" I asked.

Carmella rolled her eyes and clarified things as if I didn't understand the business, like I hadn't been running the team these past forty years. "People these days, they want excitement. Explosions. Gunfights. Sex appeal."

"Sex appeal?" I asked. "Are you crazy? Joe and I are in our sixties. There's no way to have sex appeal at our age."

She sighed and rolled her eyes, "Not you two."

"Then who?"

She ignored my question and her voice took on a lecturing tone. "You've made the iconic character of SafeCracker into an unpaid nobody."

"That's not true." I was indignant.

"Not true?" She lifted her hand and poked her index finger into my chest as she spoke. "Do ya have any current publishing contracts? Comics? Novelizations? "

"No."

"What about a pay per click serialized publication on a website somewhere?"

"You know we don't."

"What about a movie deal?"

"No."

She tried to poke me again, but I easily blocked her hand. A lifetime of martial arts training had given me mad skills. Sure I wasn't as quick or as strong as I once was, but damn if I was going to let this snip of a girl poke me in my chest.

"A TV series?" she asked

I looked at my watch. "You're wasting time with these questions."

"Do ya have… an epical?" She paused for dramatic effect, and then spoke the last word with an almost religious zeal.

I laughed at the thought, a local villain like SafeCracker had no chance of getting an epical. And that thought made me remember my schedule. "Listen, we don't have time for this."

"Yes, we do," she said.

"We're on a schedule," I said. "Professional bank robbers don't stop and have a discussion in the middle of a job."

"According to my timetable, we still have some time to waste."

When I looked over to Joe, expecting him to back me up, she poked me in the chest hard enough that I took a step backwards.

"Your plans have ruined SafeCracker."

That accusation hurt me, and she sucked me into the conversation. "Listen, you little trollop. You're coming in at the tail end of a forty year career. How many supervillians do you know that are still working after four decades?"

She laughed in my face, short, harsh, and dismissive. "That's exactly my point. In forty years, you have never hit the big time. You're a pathetic excuse for a manager. Your whole sneak-in and slip-out perspective is idiotic. There's nothing to catch the audience."

"I've kept the team safe and in the cash. I'm a good head henchman."

"You keep telling yourself that," she said with a sneer, "but the truth is you never knew the business. You're small-time because you don't think big. You're dead weight holding Joe back."

"That's not true!"

"Face it, you're only pushing for retirement because you can't manage the team anymore. You have no idea how to gain traction with the modern media. You're a washed up has been and you're dragging SafeCracker down."

"Joe?" I pleaded.

"Gene," he said, "Carmella has some new ideas. She wants to work social media. She'll get us on that app. You know the one all the kids use."

I didn't know which specific app he was talking about. There were so many and I didn't keep up with them. It wasn't necessary. The jobs we pulled these last few years were small time bank heists that kept us busy. We were just biding our time, keeping busy, while waiting for retirement.

Carmella leaned close, all sweet and nice. "SafeCracker is an iconic supervillain. All he needs is some good publicity."

"We're not looking for publicity. We've had a good run," I explained. "This is supposed to be the twilight of our careers. Joe, we're going to retire. Right?"

Joe looked me in the eye and tore my world apart. "I don't want to retire."

"But our plan?"

He waved me silent. I could see Joe's eyes were open wide in wonder and hope, like a kid about to get the toy he'd always dreamed about.

"Carmella thinks I have a chance at getting an epical," he told me, his voice almost pleading. "All the big name supers are making fortunes with this technology."

Epicals were a new kind of multi-media presentation that sent text, audio, images, animation, and video directly into a person's brain. The epical player connects to its viewer using head pads, although some people are installing wireless receivers into their skulls.

The brain perceives epicals in three-dimensions and viewers feel like they are right there in the action. Epicals also include sensory information and emotional context which blurs the line between the actors and the audience. Watching an epical is more like living through the experience.

Epicals combine video and sound files taken on site with computer generated images. Since they jack into a viewer's brain, they are perceived in three dimensions as if the person was in the action. There's an emotional overlay that enhances the viewing.

People love epicals because its an ongoing story. The producers serialize a super's life into monthly installments, capturing the highlights. It was like a comic book, but fans really felt like they were living as their heroes.

I've only used an epical once or twice. I think they ruin the experience by giving people too much detail. For me, viewing epicals causes sensory overload. I like to use my imagination, which is why I still read books.

I shook my head. "We're winding things down. Our old crew is retired. They are enjoying life, shuffling grandkids, and taking cruises."

"Epicals are a whole new industry," he insisted, sounding like the dreamer he had been thirty years ago. "I can build a whole new fan base."

"No. No." I begged. "Tell her, Joe, we're just making a little more money to retire. One more score. Then, it's off to the beach. You'll tinker with your machines. I'll learn to surf. That's been our dream for a decade."

Joe wasn't hearing me. His head was lost in fantasy. "I can hit the big time again."

The thugs, getting antsy, spread out around the van. People started to notice them brandishing their weapons, and a crowd began to gather. Many of the bystanders pulled out their phones. Some were probably calling 9-1-1, but most were shooting video in the hopes of getting something cool enough to sell.

That thought made me remember the hover cameras. They had recorded our entire conversation. I felt a little embarrassed, but I knew that the clips would never be used.

"Joe." I said, feeling like my world was coming apart. "I don't want to rob banks anymore. We had a plan. Retirement. Together. The beach. Margaritas. Doing the things we never had time to do."

From the way he fidgeted, I knew he was going to drop the bomb. As he opened his mouth to speak, I had to resist the urge to plug my ears, to shout nonsense words like I was a child again not wanting to hear something bad.

"I've reevaluated my retirement," Joe began. "When things weren't going well, I figured I should get out. But if Carmella can turn things around, then I have to give it a chance. These new epicals, they change everything."

I stood there with my mouth hanging open. I knew I must have looked pretty silly. I just couldn't close my jaw.

Joe put a hand on my shoulder. "I am a supervillain. I really love being a supervillain."

Carmella thrust herself between us. "There are newly-introduced villains making thousands of dollars from their epicals." Carmella poked me in the chest with her index finger again. "SafeCracker is a veteran villain. He is barely making ends meet. And it's all because of your mismanagement."

"Not mismanagement. Retirement. A planned downsizing." I was furious at having to defend myself to this strumpet. "We both have retirement accounts in the millions. I've set up everything. Forty years of work, so we could enjoy the fruits of our labors in our golden years. Joe and I are in our sixties. It's time to settle down."

"Gene," Carmella spoke my name like she was smelling dog crap on her shoe. "You might be a tired old man, but Joe is always ready to go." She said the last with a sly little grin and then added, "With my help, SafeCracker is going to be big time again. He's going to make a huge comeback."

"That's crazy," I told her.

"Just think of the underdog story," Joe said. "A comeback at my age."

"You're crazy." I said to Carmella. Then, I looked to my friend. "Joe?"

"Sixty is the new forty," Joe said. "I feel like a young man again."

"Hey, boss," said one of the thugs. "Are we going to go in?"

I looked at my watch. "No. Schedule's blown, back in the van. This job's a bust."

The henchmen did not move. They were not complying with my orders.

"Get back in the van." I repeated.

The thugs were looking at Carmella. She gave me a triumphant smile and flounced her hair.

"We got time," Carmella said.

"No, we don't!" I shouted, pointing at my watch.

Carmella rolled her eyes. "We are just building up to the real action."

"Building up?" I asked.

"Sure," she said, pointing causally to the crowd gathering on the sidewalks. She waved to them. "The longer we wait, the more people will see us."

"The cops will be coming," I said. "We have to be in and out before that."

She shook her head. "That's why we are waiting. Conflicts with cops will increase our exposure."

"They'll be shooting at us."

"And we'll be shooting back."

"We don't work this way. This isn't our style." I hated the way my voice sounded. I was pleading. "We can't do this. People are going to get hurt."

"The modern audience expects some violence." Joe said.

"Actually," Carmella added in a know-it-all tone, "violence is required."

Her tone pissed me off. "So we hurt the cops for ratings."

"You're catching on," Carmella said.

Joe frowned. "It's different now. In our day, people respected the police. Kids looked up to them. They were valued by everyone. Times change."

"That's nuts," I scoffed. After forty years of being head henchman, I was not going to beg for Joe to listen. "Police officers are hard working people with families who do a very important job."

Carmella poked me again. "Everyone knows cops are authoritarian jerks."

"Hurting them is wrong."

"Don't bring morality into this," she retorted. "It's all about demographics. Our target audience loves when supervillains lay a beat-down on the boys in blue."

I threw my hands in the air. "This is madness. Next you'll be telling me we should be fighting superheroes."

"Absolutely!" Her smile was wide and dangerous. "Years ago, villains had to be careful not to beat a hero. That's not true anymore. Today's audience likes to cheer for the villain. They enjoy seeing stuck-up heroes get the beat down."

I sighed. There was some truth to what Carmella was saying. I didn't understand the phenomena, but people didn't value heroes like they did in the last century. Back then, people wanted good to triumph over evil or they didn't like the story. Villains were just extras that made the heroes look good, and those who bucked the system often had their careers ruined.

When Joe and I started, the big-power villains would often monologue to give the heroes who faced them an opportunity to succeed. Back then, villains spent most of their time trying to make sure that the hero looked good, because that's what the audience wanted.

The villains who beat heroes would restrain them in some kind of death trap. They would tie them to train tracks or lock them in a room with a bomb. But the villain purposely designed the trap with a flaw that let the hero escape.

The old audiences loved the monologues and the death traps that aways failed, but Carmella was right. Modern audiences would see through that fiction. Nowadays, villains could be characters in their own right. Many of them had large followings. The audience accepted their villainy as long as the bad acts were justified by a tragic childhood or some other often-invented angst. Still, just because the audience has changed didn't mean we should go looking for trouble.

A showdown with a superhero was a bit beyond our current status. I would not be able to handle any of the active supers in our city. Sure, in my youth, I could have gone punch for punch with most heroes, but we didn't. We avoided other supers, like we avoided the cops. It was just smart business to play it safe and reap in the cash from the heist.

I was still lost in thought, pining for the old days, when Carmella announced loudly, "Let's go, boys. Time to put SafeCracker back on top. Shock and awe. Flash and flare."

I had no choice. I had to follow. A professional didn't bail in the middle of a job, no matter how many things went wrong.

According to my schedule, we should already be piling back in the van and racing away. Instead, we were heading up the steps following Carmella's swinging hips. My every instinct screamed run, run, run. This was total folly, but I was loyal to Joe. When this job went bad, like I knew it would, he'd need me by his side.

Chapter Three

The First National Bank building was a massive monument of white marble with wide steps leading up to immense bronze doors. Tall narrow windows set high up from the street guided the eye to a Roman style peaked roof with soaring eagles carved in bas-relief.

The hover cameras circled us as I opened the right door and Carmella got the left. SafeCracker strode between us, entering the bank, looking magnificent. Confident, back straight, chin up, cape flowing, he always made his entrance in style. He was still an iconic supervillain, even after all these years.

"Everyone on the floor," I shouted, in my best tough guy voice.

Most got right down as we crossed the lobby, but some hesitated and the thugs rushed to get control of the room, which was exactly what they were hired to do. The key to every successful bank heist was managing the customers and employees.

"On the floor!" One of our thugs screamed at a woman in a tight skirt.

She obviously didn't want to lay down in such a scanty garment and was trying to kneel while maintaining some decency. The thug clubbed her with the stock of his rifle. The woman dropped to the floor.

His actions infuriated me. I was hotter than I'd ever been on a mission, but I forced myself to be calm as I rushed over to check on the woman. She was unconscious, but breathing steady. I felt her skull. A small lump, nothing more, but head injuries were always dangerous.

"I said no violence."

"Uggh," The thug hesitated. "Carmella said to club anyone who didn't immediately obey."

"You don't hit women."

"That's sexist," the thug said.

"We don't hit anyone!"

"But..."

I cut him off. "I am the top thug on this team. You listen to me!"

He gave me a sulky nod.

"Secure the room!" I said, promising myself to address the thug's breach of professional etiquette after the mission. That thug's brutality had just lost him his job. He was getting fired as soon as we got back to the hideout. No way was he staying on this team.

Back in the day, everyone followed the comic code. People respected each other and kept the violence to a minimum. Minions always treated civilians with respect and civilians didn't interfere. They stayed clear of the action. We made sure they didn't get hurt. It was a sensible, unspoken understanding that kept everyone safe and made our jobs a lot easier.

The cops would arrive on the scene, but they also understood their role was to arrest the everyday criminals. Being a cop was hard enough, and they were not trained to tangle with super powers. Most would sensibly wait for the experts to show up, and then step aside. Superheroes fought supervillains, and everyone enjoyed the action.

On the other side of the lobby, a thug shouted at a teenage girl, "Eat that floor."

The kid looked up with a blank stare, totally confused, acting like she didn't know the bank was being robbed. Then I understood, she had been too absorbed, staring at her phone, to even notice our entrance. The thug shoved her down to the floor by holding the back of her neck. She squirmed and cried out. He was a little too rough, but at least he didn't club her.

"On the floor," I repeated, proud of my tough-guy voice, and the effect I had on people.

Everyone was down on the floor except for an old lady with a walker standing near the rest room and two big dudes standing at the teller windows.

I sighed seeing the problem in the cocksure way the two big dudes stared at SafeCracker as if sizing him up. One had a black cowboy hat. The other had a white one. Both had boots made out of some kind of lizard skin.

"Hey, get down!" I called.

Their eyes shifted to me, and I knew immediately this was going to be real trouble if not handled correctly.

"You feel like gettin' down, Dave?" asked the cowboy in the black hat.

"Well, Dan." The cowboy with the white hat spoke in a slow drawl. "I don't reckon' I do."

I crossed the lobby to them. Back in the day, when a villain walked into a bank people hurried to the floor. The wearing of a costume was enough to earn respect. Back then, spectators were happy to watch the show. And believe me, a well-planned robbery was fun to see.

Nowadays, you had to watch for people like the guys at the teller window. If you didn't have a well-known super power or a nasty reputation, some civilian might jump you. Most were people seeking five minutes of fame on the news channel, but some thought they were doing the right thing. Either way, spectators jumping in was a new problem supervillains needed to address.

"You looking for trouble?" I asked confidently.

"I don't expect you'll give us much trouble," Dan spoke, pushing himself off the counter and drawing himself up to his full height which caused him to tower over me.

I briefly considered calling the thugs over to handle them. I didn't really want to throw down with a pair of rednecks half my age, but then Dave called me, "Pops."

Now I've been called a lot of bad names on the job, and I never took it personally, but the way that kid spoke down to me really lit my fuse.

I chopped Dave in the throat. Then, ducked down so Dan punched over my head. He got a gut punch for his effort and as he folded over my fist, I rose up using the back of my head to smash his face. Dan fell backwards, landing unconscious on the floor.

Still choking from my knife-hand to his throat, Dave grabbed my shoulder. Dumb move. I gave him two quick left jabs to the cheek which disoriented him, and then knocked him out with a right cross to his chin.

The whole fight took seconds, and I could see the thugs staring at me in awe. Even Carmella looked a little impressed.

"Focus on the mission," I snapped and the thugs hastened to their tasks.

The old woman who was standing with her walker by the rest room had still not found the floor. She looked to be in her eighties, and I would have let her stay standing as she was clearly having trouble getting down, but Carmella was heading toward her like a shark swimming towards its next meal.

"You better get down, hag." Carmella shouted continuing to close the distance.

The elderly lady saw Carmella coming and redoubled her efforts. With both hands on her walker, the poor woman kept trying to lower herself but her knees were all wobbly. I was afraid she'd fall and break a hip. Of course, if Carmella reached her a broken hip might be the least of her injuries.

I sprinted to arrive at the old woman first. "I'll take care of this one."

Carmella scowled. "You looking for a date?"

"You're supposed to be going for the vault." I retorted.

She opened her mouth to reply, but before she could make some sarcastic retort SafeCracker called to her from the hall leading to the vault. He stood with the bank manager, and was clearly waiting on her. She flounced away.

I gently took hold of the old woman's arm with one hand. "I'm so sorry."

"Things look a bit chaotic," she said, leaning her weight on me. I wrapped my other arm around her waist, amazed at how light and frail she felt in my arms.

"Yep."

Carmella waved her pistol in the bank manager's face calling him a string of foul-mouthed curses. I could still hear their echoes as she disappeared down the hall with SafeCracker.

Two of the thugs cleaned out the cash drawers at the teller stations, while the remaining three roamed the floor keeping everyone down.

"My knees don't work like they used to," she said.

"Neither do mine," I commiserated.

"Wait until you're my age," she said.

Even with my help, the poor old woman could not kneel down. Her legs started shaking uncontrollably as she tried to comply.

At this rate, she'd just drop to the floor. I didn't want that.

"Wait," I told her.

She continued to struggle. "I can do it."

"Stop," I said firmly. "I have a better idea."

"Let me help you to a chair. This robbery might take a while."

She held onto her walker, exhausted from her efforts. "Maybe you could just bring the chair to me."

"Sure." I pulled a chair over.

"Thank you," she said. "I just don't have any strength in my legs. Everything is downhill after fifty."

"It's okay," I said. "I understand."

"I'm sure you do," she said sweetly. "You ain't no spring chicken yourself."

"No ma'am, I'm not."

"Your team always had class," she said. "Lots of class and character."

"Are you a fan of SafeCracker?"

"Absolutely," She peered at me through her spectacles.

I was not surprised that she recognized us. SafeCracker had a sizable following back in the day. There was a time when I had to allocate precious minutes during our heists to autograph signing.

"Honey." She patted my arm. "I loved the SafeCracker series. I'd read your comics to my kids before bed. I still have a few of your books around somewhere."

"Thank you." Fans always made me feel good.

"You are welcome," she gushed. "I remember the SafeCracker comic. In Issue #14, you boys used a stolen Lamborghini as your getaway car. You jumped the bay bridge when it was open and got away from that big-name superhero. I forget his name."

"LavaStorm," I supplied.

"Yes! He kept trying to hit you with balls of magma, but you kept dodging."

"The Lamborghini had excellent handling."

"You were a great driver!" she said. "You always did crazy things with cars. Remember when you got away from WindRunner by driving up onto the automobile carrier. He flew right by and didn't realize. After he was gone, you backed off the carrier and just drove away. That was classic SafeCracker."

"Those were the good days," I said.

"Sure were. These new heroes don't have the old style. Hasn't been the same in this city since LavaStorm and WindRunner both retired."

I shrugged. "Vortex is pretty cool."

She agreed, then asked, "You still got a comic?"

"No," I admitted.

She patted my arm. "Things change."

"Sure do," I said, remembering how much I loved to drive the getaway car, but I gave it up about a decade ago when my reaction time slowed and my vision declined. I didn't want to run into someone accidentally. It was safer to hire a young driver. My vision was so bad these days that I avoided driving at night.

"Life changes, but you'll always have your memories. Age cannot take away the good times. I still remember the way you outsmarted all those more powerful supers."

"We did what we could with what we had."

The lady laughed. "And you always told good stories, too."

I was responsible for creating much of the drama around Joe's SafeCracker image. As the head henchman, I had a lot of contact with the comic writers. Joe's main super power gave him control over machines. That's not a flashy power so we needed character and depth to attract our fans. Which was fine because Joe and I wanted our comic to be about the people on the team. We wanted everyone to share their story, the good and the bad, so I made sure the writers blended our larger-than-life antics with our mundane everyday lives.

Our story was about people. We gave the audience spectacular heists, but we also shared aspects of our day to day lives. The fans got to see the relationship between a supervillain and his top thug. They read about our team members. They followed the marriages, the divorces, and how they struggled to raise their kids. It was a unique read at the time, and very popular until life broke up the old gang.

"You and SafeCracker always did it right. These new villains are too flashy and violent. They hurt people and wreck things. You boys never did that. Old-time villains had style."

"Yes, we did."

"And you took your lumps. Doing your time and always completing your community service."

It felt good to know we still had a few fans. I was happy for the vindication of our career. People still remembered and appreciated how we had always tried to do the right thing. Villains didn't have to be bad people.

She laid a hand on my arm and said, "I think you boys are the last of the classic villains to still be active."

"We are."

"The new villains all think the story is about them," she said. "But it shouldn't be. The heroes should always be the protagonist. Stories should inspire people to be better. Villains should be the bad guys that people love to hate."

"Things are a little jumbled in the industry," I said.

She frowned. "Things are jumbled everywhere. People idolizing villains. Back in the day, everyone wanted to be a hero. I don't know what's wrong with these kids. Why cheer for the criminal? What's the world coming to?"

I shrugged. The way I looked at it was that if it wasn't for us supervillains, then the world wouldn't have superheroes. Every story needs the antagonist, and we played our role as best we could.

She patted my arm and said, "You're too good for this world. You might want to think about retirement."

"It's been discussed," I said.

"Do supervillains have retirement accounts?"

"We do."

I checked the room. The lobby was still secure, two thugs on the door with the cash from the teller station in sacks over their shoulders, two thugs on the floor, and one roaming thug. Carmella had accompanied Joe to the vault. Everything was going according to the original plan. I started to relax. We were just seriously behind schedule because of our sidewalk discussion.

"The rest of your team retired years ago, didn't they?" she asked

"Yes." I needed to focus on the job.

"Don't waste your golden years working," the woman said. "Take it from me. I didn't start living until I retired. I spent my whole life teaching in public education. I considered staying until sixty or even sixty-five, but retiring at fifty-five was the best thing I ever did."

"I understand," I said, only half listening because I needed to keep an eye on the thugs.

"You have something special planned?" she asked.

"Yeah," I said.

"Tell me."

I didn't want to be rude, so I told her the retirement dream Joe and I planned years ago. "House on the beach. Listening to the ocean roll over the sand and learning how to surf."

"Sounds like you got it all figured out. What's keeping you here?"

She must have seen my eyes drift back to the vault.

"Oh, you got loyalties."

I nodded.

"Not that horrible girl."

"No." I laughed.

"You listen to me," said the lady, squeezing my arm. "I had a good friend. I taught with her for years, we always planned to do things together, but she kept teaching till sixty-five. She retired and a year later she died. We never got to do all the things we talked about. Life is too precious to waste working."

"I'll keep that in mind."

She seemed to recognize I was waffling. She fixed me with a steely gaze. "You both need to retire. If SafeCracker doesn't go, then you go."

"Take care," I said to the woman

She waggled her finger at me as I started to turn away. "You listen to me. I know how fast the years go by. Decades in a blink."

I never got to reply. The staccato sound of an assault rifle firing in three long bursts drowned out anything I planned to say.

Chapter Four

With plaster chunks raining down around her, Carmella charged into the main chamber of the bank from a side hall. She fired another long burst into the ceiling. The bank costumers screamed, covered their ears, and pressed their faces to the floor. More chunks of the ceiling fell and plaster dust floated down like fine mist.

I rushed to Carmella. "What are you doing?"

"Getting their attention."

Aghast, I looked up at the beautiful vaulted ceiling marred by bullet holes. "This building is over a hundred years old."

She squeezed off another long burst shattering a few of the high glass windows on the front of the building. She probably would have done more damage, but the bolt locked back indicating the magazine was empty.

"That was not necessary," I said.

"Quiet, pops. I got this."

I was too stunned to be angry.

"Listen up, you bitches," shouted Camilla waving the empty gun. "I want all your rocks. Take them off your fingers and give them to my boys."

It took me a few moments to understand what she was saying. "You can't take their jewelry!"

"Watch me."

One of our thugs was pulling an engagement ring from a crying young woman.

"Don't do this, Carmella," I was trying to keep my voice low. "Taking the bank's money isn't personal, but you're hurting these people. That jewelry has sentimental value."

"Pipe down, pops," Carmella told me. "The boss told you about changes to the plan. This is one of them."

"Where is SafeCracker?"

"He's popping the safe deposit boxes." Camella jammed a new magazine into her assault rifle.

"How many boxes is he opening?"

"I told him to keep going until he finds something worth our time."

"You..? You don't tell the boss what to do."

She popped a gum bubble in my face.

"Hitting the boxes takes too much time," I shouted, appalled by the sheer idiocy of the situation.

She blew another big bubble with her gum. It burst with a loud snap. "We got time."

"The cops are going to be here!"

She looked at me like I was an idiot. "I know. That's why we are still here."

"You can't be serious." My head was spinning. "We're going to have to shoot our way out."

"Exactly," she said, with the widest of smiles.

I had to get away from her before I did something I would regret. In all my years of managing minions, I'd never wanted to beat one senseless. I ran toward the vault, and by the time I found Joe in the safe deposit room I was mostly calm, but I needed a few more deep breaths to be sure, so I watched my friend work.

SafeCracker opened the boxes one box at a time. I never really understood his power. He just pressed his index finger against the lock and held it there, jiggling the tumblers by twisting his wrist. After a short time, the lock just opened up.

A scientist tested Joe once and said that he was able to manipulate some kind of fundamental energy. These forces are responsible for physics. Reality is defined by energies, and people who can manipulate them can do impossible things. Last I heard, scientists had identified fifteen or sixteen major energies and some minor ones as well. It's a developing discipline. Some people think it's old world magic; others discount it as a scam. I really don't know. Some people have super powers while others don't. That's just how it is.

"Joe, what are you doing?" I asked.

"Banks don't keep much money in the vault anymore, so the only way we can really score is by hitting the safe deposit boxes."

"Forget the boxes," I said. "What are you doing with Carmella?"

"She says the boxes will have lots of jewelry and she is right." He pointed to the sack next to him.

"Are you with her?"

"With her?" he asked. Then, he understood. "Heavens no. She's a minion. That's against the code." He reached out and touched my arm. "You know I'd never do that."

I let out the breath I didn't realize I'd been holding. "We're four minutes and twenty-two seconds over time. We have to go!"

"One more box."

I wanted to tell him no, but he was the villain, and it was his decision.

I stood there alternately looking at him, and then looking at the sweep hand of my watch tick past the numbers on the dial. The seconds were adding up to big jail time.

"I think Carmella wants a standoff with the cops."

"No standoff," he said. "The plan is to burst out, makes a scene, and then meet up with Frank at the alternate pick-up location."

I didn't know how that harpy had convinced him of this crazy plan.

"You think that's a good idea?"

Instead of replying, he opened the box. "Damn. Only papers. Maybe one more."

Joe started to pop open another.

I heard the sirens, so did Joe.

"The cops are here," I said.

"Yeah." He stood up. "That means it's show time."

I followed him back to the lobby, where I found Carmella arguing with the old lady who I had been talking to. "Give me your wedding rings, or I put one between your eyes."

"You're not stealing my rings. My husband, rest his soul, gave them to me. I've worn them for fifty-two years. They're a part of my life."

The woman was not afraid, and I think that made Carmella angrier than her refusal to give up the rings.

"You ain't gonna have a life if you don't hand 'em over." Carmella placed the barrel of her gun against the woman's wrinkled brow. The oldster didn't even flinch. I didn't know if Carmella was bluffing or not. I grabbed the barrel of her assault rifle and wrenched it away. I pushed the barrel to the ceiling and looked Carmella right in the eyes. She met my gaze. She'd not been bluffing.

"You and Joe might have talked about changing plans, but I'm still the head henchman." I pulled the cloth bag of stolen jewelry out of Carmella's hand and handed it to the elderly woman. "Please see that these items are returned."

"Bless your heart."

"That ain't happening." Carmella shook my hand off the barrel of the gun with a few sideways jerks.

"I'm in charge," I said, firmly.

The fury on her face scared me. I stepped back. Coming between her and money was like coming between a rabid dog and raw meat. She reached for the bag, probably intending to rip it out of the old woman's trembling hand.

Recovering, I grabbed Carmella's wrist. "No."

She struggled to pull free, looking surprised to find my grip so strong. I may be old, but I'm no pushover. The years of jogging, weight lifting, and martial arts had let me keep my strength. I was not going to let Carmella bully this woman.

Her eyes narrowed, her lips pulled back from her teeth. She looked like a blood-thirsty predator getting ready to pounce. The barrel of her gun began to lower. She was going to shoot me and then probably shoot the old woman. I was seeing the true Carmella, a creature that had no morals or scruples who would do anything to get her way.

"You can have my share of the cash."

For a moment, Carmella didn't understand.

"My share is worth more than this jewelry. Take my share and let's get out of here."

The descent of the muzzle stopped, she was calculating her options and money was a language she could understand. On many teams, the head henchman kept order with threats of violence. In my forty plus years of robbing banks, I never had to threaten a member of the team. This was breaking my heart, betraying the codes I held dear.

I saw the greed in her eyes. "I could have both."

"I won't die easy." I said.

She smiled, and laughed it off. "I'll take your share. We'll let grandma keep the baubles."

The tires squealing on the street in front of the bank was a bad sign. SafeCracker looked out the window. "Cops have closed the street."

"That's good," Carmella said.

"Good?" Had she gone insane?

"Franky's gone down the block," Joe said. "He's in the backup position."

At least someone had followed the plan. It was my standing procedure that if the cops came, the getaway driver would pull away and park in the designated secondary location. In this case, Franky should be waiting for us in an alley, two streets down.

"The escape plan is up to the roof." I reminded them. "We run down the block jumping from roof to roof. Use the fire escape on the corner store to reach the street. Then, we run to Franky and burn rubber out of here."

"That's not the plan anymore," Carmella said, stopping me in my tracks. "We're going out the front."

"That's not our style," I said.

"Listen, old man," she replied. "I'm running this show."

"If we go out the front, they will start shooting."

My fears were not her fears. She laughed. "Those cops, they got pistols. We've got assault rifles. That gives us the advantage of firepower."

"That's not the point," I said.

Carmella smiled so sweetly and batted her eyes. "It'll be easy."

"We can't have a shootout!" I said. "And every second we waste allows more cops to arrive. They will spread out and block off the area. Let's get to the roof."

The thugs were assembling at the front door, making sure their guns were on full auto, and zipping their Kevlar armor up around their necks. This delay had all been planned. I had a sinking feeling in my chest.

"No. No," I said to Joe. "You have to stop this. We go low key. We slip in and slip out."

"Carmella's got new ideas," said Joe, obviously trying to make peace.

"They're not new ideas," I pleaded. "They're rookie mistakes. Things we learned not to do years ago. Gunfights with the police were always something we avoided."

"This is a new era," Joe said. "Villains need to be confrontational to get the spotlight."

"That's Carmella's nonsense," I argued.

"It's the new way. Look at the blockbuster movies with all the explosions. That's what people want from their superstars. We need action. We need shock and awe."

"A gunfight with the cops won't get you an epical."

Joe waved me silent. "The goal is not a gunfight."

"Then what the hell are we doing?" I demanded.

"We have to go out the front because Carmella is going to announce herself as a supervillain."

"What?" I could not believe what I was hearing.

"Get ready boys!" Carmella shouted to our thugs.

I grabbed Joe's arm. "She's not a supervillain."

"She is," Joe assured me. "Watch and see."

"She's a thug. An up-jumped thug."

Joe turned away, walking toward the bronze doors, leaving me speaking to the empty air where he had been standing. That hurt more than anything. In all the years we worked together, Joe had never ignored my suggestions, never dismissed me like I was nothing.

"This is wrong boss," I shouted, running after him. "People are going to get hurt."

As I reached the doors, Carmella spun on me. She shoved me,

hard. I stumbled backward and almost fell.

"Your days of leading this team to ruin are over. You see those news vans?" She pointed through the bank windows. "They're looking for stuff worth watching. They want action and strong characters. They want a spectacle, and we're going to give them one. We're going to walk out those doors and show the world SafeCracker still has his balls. And we're going to show them a brand-new supervillain."

"This is all wrong." I pleaded.

"You're just not getting it, Pops. Let me show you." Carmella passed her assault rifle to a thug and then pulled off her black ski mask revealing her long red hair. Covering her cheeks and eyes was one of those modern supervillain masks, the kind that stuck to your face without a strap behind the head. It was sleek and black and had a silver sheen. She unzipped her plain-grey henchman coat and let it slide from her shoulders. She undid the buckle on her belt and let her baggy henchman pants drop down to her ankles. My eyes followed the pants down and then back up. She was wearing a tight-fitting black supervillain costume accented with small silver keys, lock tumbles, and gears. Around her waist was a sleek fitting utility belt with a half dozen small pouches.

She stepped away from her henchman costume and looked at me. "I'm BankJob, and this is my announcement to the world."

Chapter Five

I stared at Carmella. My mouth must have been hanging open for at least a dozen heartbeats. Finally, I recovered my wits enough to say, "But you don't have super powers."

She laughed scornfully. "You don't know a thing about me."

I wanted to say that I knew everything necessary, but she talked right over me.

"I'm a super-apothecary. Building and using amazing chemical compounds is my specialty. I don't expect a geezer like you to understand super-tech."

I understood plenty. I wanted to object to her costume, to her plan, to her name, to everything. I could do none of it. Time had run out. Our thugs were pushing open the front doors and blazing away with their automatic weapons. I heard two huge explosions. Grenades? Our thugs were throwing grenades. Where the hell did they get grenades?

Carmella strutted through the open doors, making a grand entrance into her new life as a supervillain. Two flaming police cruisers cast their shimmering light onto her costume. She walked down the steps, hair blowing in the wind. Joe followed in her wake with the thugs three steps behind.

Carmella was right about one thing, the pistols didn't stand a chance against the automatic guns. Our thugs were hosing down the street with a fusillade of lead. It was more than overkill. It was Hollywood style gratuitous violence. The kind of stuff Joe and I had always avoided. Three cops lay sprawled on the ground. I hoped they'd not been hurt too badly. The rest were hiding behind the second line of police cruisers keeping their heads down as bullets pounded around them.

The half-dozen news vans parked behind the police cars buzzed with activity. Hover cameras from the local news agencies buzzed all around us. Reporters spoke into their microphones as their camera persons captured the action with handheld cameras. Spectators lined the streets holding up cell phones. A person could sell a photo or video of a super for thousands of dollars.

I waited for a few more seconds then started down. A few bullets bounced off my Kevlar chest plate as I descended to the street. I felt the sting and knew my chest would be bruised tomorrow.

Carmella stopped on the sidewalk with burning police cars to either side. She kicked a hip out to her left and held the gun upwards. Hover cameras zipped in to capture her likeness.

Catching up to her I asked, "Are you posing?"

She ignored me.

"Henchmen don't pose." I persisted.

"Honey," she told me. "In case you haven't noticed, I am a henchman no more."

"A costume doesn't make a super." I said. "You need super powers."

"I got everything I need right here." I couldn't tell if she was patting her ass or the equipment utility belt around her waist.

Carmella walked between the two burning police cars, firing from the hip and spraying the second line of police cruisers with bullets. Windshields and side windows exploded. Bullet holes punched through steel leaving little silver holes. Cops huddled behind engine blocks hoping not to get shot.

I followed her, shouting, "What are you doing?"

"Those ball-lickers gotta learn to respect me!"

I grabbed her arm, the one she was using to guide the barrel back and forth over the cars. "No!"

She shrugged me off.

"You could kill someone."

"Get with the times," she shouted. "The fans want this. Trust me, these days people hate cops more than they hate criminals."

She pointed to the cheering crowds. Many had their phones out in front of their faces. They were getting video.

Carmella laughed and shook her had, cascading her hair for the cameras. "The more explosions. The more violence. The more cops getting hurt. The more people like it."

"This is wrong."

"The comic industry has changed."

"The code..."

"Is gone,"she cut me off. "You're too soft to make money in the modern world, old man."

She strode away, red hair trailing behind like a halo of fire.

Once again, I stood there with my mouth open. Shocked, staring after her. She was one beautiful woman. No. Her beauty was just on the outside. Underneath that perfectly toned body and glamour-girl face was a darkly unpleasant core. She was an ugly, ugly woman.

"Shoot 'em up, boys," she called to the thugs. "Blast anything or anyone who gets in our way."

Our thugs happily blazed away at the SWAT van as it approached. The windshield spider-webbed and predictably the driver lost control and ran into a fire hydrant. Water shot up into the sky. The cops staggered out as bullets slammed into their body armor, knocking them to the ground.

I ran after Carmella. "No. No. Why would you tell them that?"

She fixed me her 'why are you so stupid' look. "When you shoot at them, they take you more serious."

"When you shoot at them, they shoot back," I said.

She didn't even listen.

Carmella leaped up on a police cruiser. She waved to the reporters and the camera operators. "Come on over."

Tentatively, they began to gather around. The cops stopped shouting. Courtesy required that a supervillain be allowed to monologue, so Carmella stood there in the afternoon light with the geyser of water from the broken hydrant giving her a spectacular backdrop.

"Listen up, folks," she yelled. "There is a new villain in town, and her name is BankJob. SafeCracker is making a comeback! All you wanna-be superhero shit-bags with your big money deals. We're calling you out. Just try and stop us."

I was going to let her have her moment, but now she was dragging Joe into her insanity. I climbed up on the roof of the police cruiser next to her.

"What the hell are you doing?" I demanded.

"Get down," she said.

"SafeCracker is not calling anyone out," I shouted to the reporters.

"Yes, he is," Carmella shouted.

"You're not even a real super," I insisted. "You're a henchman. You're a thug who works for me."

If looks could kill, I'd be a dead man.

"Shut the hell up," she hissed. "This is my moment."

I tried to pull her off the police cruiser's roof. Dumb move. My footing was poor. She shook me off and gave me a little shove. I bounced down the windshield, slid off the hood, and landed hard on the ground. Luckily, I didn't break a hip.

"Are you bros and bitches getting this?" she shouted to the professional camera operators. "I am BankJob."

The reporters surged forward waving their microphones and shouting questions.

"What are your super abilities?"

"Who made your costume?"

"Are you and SafeCracker a couple?"

"Listen up, all you super suckers," she shouted over them. "All you boot licking, brown-noses who cater to your movie producers and print publishers, it's time to face a real villain. You've fought against second-rate try-hards for too long. It's time to prove your street cred and be real heroes.

"You rep-out as action junkies, but BankJob and SafeCracker are going to show the paying public what you truly are… clueless, overpaid, chumps. That's right. I said it. You heard it. BankJob is born. SafeCracker is back. And we're better than all of you pathetic poseurs in every way."

Carmella did a back flip off the cruiser and landed on one knee with the opposite fist on the pavement next to her knee. She paused for a moment, holding the classic overdone superhero pose as people snapped her photo. What a show-off. She hopped to her feet and sprinted up the street spraying storefronts with bursts of lead. The windows shattered, and spectators ran for cover. It was all such a needless waste.

Back in the day, you didn't break windows for no reason. Sure, you might jump out a window to make an escape. Hey, you might throw a superhero through a window to make a point. Carmella was just breaking the windows to cause damage. This kind of activity was the same kind of ignorant as shooting up road signs. I hated it and if I could have stopped her, I would have, but I had my own problems.

The cops were running toward me with cuffs dangling in their fists. They were pissed off and looking for blood. I knew if they got their hands on me, I was going to catch a pretty good beating. I jumped up and tried to follow my team down the road. Limping along on my aching knees, I wondered how many years I would get for Carmella's gratuitous violence.

The cops had almost reached me, when a news bureau's camera copter zoomed down directly overhead. I'm sure the cops would have caught me if not for the rotor wash. The spinning props blew smoke and kicked up burning pieces of the police cars. Most of it whirled onto the street covering the cops who choked and patted at their uniforms to extinguish the sparks landing on them. My fire retardant henchman uniform protected me so I didn't need to worry.

I took advantage of my good fortune to run as fast as I could, which was not as fast as it had been in the days of my youth. I was getting too old for this. Years ago, I didn't mind running from the cops every once in a while. A good chase broke the monotony of a perfect heist.

As I raced down the street, I kept thinking about the old days when comics were making a huge comeback, and everyone was trying to cash in on the super craze. Most people came by their powers accidentally through exposure to chemicals, cosmic rays, or some other definitive event. Some experimented on their bodies, while others used gadgets to augment their normal human forms. There were even a few robots and non-corporeal entities.

Into this esteemed collection, entered Joe. His super power allowed him to control machines. He could touch any lock with his index finger and have it pop open in just a few minutes. It was not much of a super power, not in a world where superhumans could fly, shoot power beams, control the weather, and all sorts of really cool stuff, but we didn't let that hold us back.

We were just two dreamers sitting around my mother's dining room table when I suggested the plan. We'd break into supermarkets after hours and he'd pop open their safes. We did this for years, all over the state. We slowly built our nest egg, always planning for the day we could sew together some costumes and gather a crew.

Joe and I started our bank-robbing career at the perfect time. We hit at the height of the comic book craze when publishers were paying millions to the lucky supers who captured the hearts and minds of their readers. SafeCracker stood out in a world of uber-powered supers, a simple guy with a simple power, making the best of his life.

Our team was an ensemble cast full of interesting characters, so I took the human angle for our stories. The readers loved following our day-to-day lives, just as much as they embraced the daring bank robberies we pulled off. We had some really good years when the sales of our comics were more than the money from our robberies, but nothing lasts forever. One by one the members of our team left the life.

Joe and I loved the life, but after the turn of the century, the industry changed. Comic book sales fell off. Super-fans became other fans and costumed heroes and villains shared the spotlight with so many other competing interests from computer games to reality television to live-action roleplaying.

We lost our publishing contract and didn't have a comic anymore. Joe and I kept busy, planning a few jobs, but never got back into the big time. Banks even started storing less money in their vaults so we had to branch out into other kinds of robberies.

The comic boom of the 90s gave way to an era of blockbuster movies and big-time money where you either made it or didn't. There wasn't a lot of room for old-timers like us, not when you had so many young people using Internet promotion and streaming videos to attract their audiences.

We started looking into other lines of work, all criminal of course. It's not like either of us wanted to join the workforce. His super skill opened locks, but it also manipulated machines. He could easily control anything with gears, tumblers, pistons, or levers, but as the influence of technology expanded he began experimenting with computers. Joe discovered that his power over machines included robots and other devices controlled by circuitry and programming.

We often talked about exploring the full panoply of his powers, but we'd always fallen back to robbing banks. That's what we knew. It was our comfort zone, and honestly, I didn't want more. I'd had my glory and forty years of fun with my friends. It was time to get out.

The camera copter paced me traveling just above street level. They were getting a good shot of Carmella's backside as she ran up the street to the waiting van. I was concerned that my team would pull away without me. Clearly Carmella wanted to, but Joe was having none of that. He shoved her into the vehicle and waved emphatically to me. Somehow, I found a burst of speed. I jumped in and slammed the sliding door. Seeing Carmella sitting smugly in the head henchman seat was just icing on my cake of my misery.

Franky was all hyped up. "Are you ready to ride?"

No one replied, and he shouted. "Come on, are you ready for a ride?"

"Drive you asshole," Carmella said.

"You have to say the line." His eyes were wide and bloodshot.

Carmella slapped him on the back of the head. "Punch it, Franky, or I'll shoot you in the head and drive myself."

"That's not the line."

Carmella lifted her gun. Franky trounced down on the gas pedal, and the van accelerated. The big engine roared and there was even some tire spinning. The van was geared for pulling heavy loads and not for fast get-a-ways. I liked vans because they weren't flashy. No one looked twice at a plain white cargo van. A team who did a job right didn't need to make a fast get-away. They could just cruise off into anonymity with no fuss or muss. Of course, that wasn't going to happen today.

Franky kept the pedal mostly to the floor. He made a few turns and negotiated city traffic by bouncing up on the sidewalk when necessary. Then he took the entrance ramp to the highway running through the center of the city. Soon, the van was streaking down the mostly empty road at a get-away speed with half a dozen cop cars chasing and the news copter zooming overhead.

"Now what are you going to do, BankJob?" I asked Carmella, smugly. We wouldn't get out of this. There was definitely going to be some prison time over this bungled mess.

"I'll show you, old man." She climbed over the seat, pushed her way through the thugs, and opened both back doors. She waved to the camera operator on the news helicopter. Was she telling him to get a close-up?

Carmella reached into one of the pockets on her utility belt and removed a hand full of little silver disks. I'd seen a few of them laying around Joe's workshop. I didn't take notice as Joe was always tinkering with old clocks and mechanical devices.

She made a show of tossing the silver disks onto the road behind our van. The copter got a great shot of her and it irked me that she was doing super stuff. SafeCracker should be doing everything cool. The henchman's job was to make the villain look good. She was stealing the spotlight, that wasn't how things worked.

But then again, Carmella was wearing a super's costume, so I guess maybe she thought it was okay for her to steal the show. Was I supposed to make her look good? No way. I considered hopping from my seat and giving her a shove out the back. That would certainly give her a starring role in a viral blooper video and probably save us by stopping the pursuit. Those cops would be all over her after what she said. I resisted the urge, and stayed true to the henchman-villain code.

The front tire on the lead police cruiser hit one of the silver disks which exploded, ripping the whole wheel off the car. The driver lost control, turned sideways, and the second car slammed into its side. Both cars came to a grinding halt.

The four following cruisers swerved wildly to avoid piling up against the two lead cars. More tires exploded as they hit the disks. Spark flew up from the asphalt as the vehicles slid along the highway on their undercarriages. I could see the faces of the panicked drivers as they fought to control their speeding cars.

One vehicle flipped over. One slammed into a tree on the side of the road. At least the other two managed to stop without hitting anything. The thugs cheered. Carmella blew them kisses. I just felt sick and worried, hoping the officers were not too badly injured.

A police chopper appeared overhead, pushing in front of the camera copter. The officer spoke through a powerful speaker, "Pull over."

Carmella reached under the rear seat and pulled out a rocket launcher. Where the hell did she get one of those? More important, why didn't I know about it? She leaned out of the van, holding onto the roof with one hand, and balancing on the bumper.

"Keep it steady, Franky!" She aimed the rocket launcher with one arm.

The officer flying the helicopter must have seen the danger. He veered away, but that was probably what Carmella was waiting for.

She fired the rocket as the copter turned broadside in its attempt to flee. She couldn't miss. The shot hit the fuselage, exploding against the metal and knocking the copter sideways in the sky.

Flaming debris rained down. The copter whirled around as the pilot struggled for control. For a few heart pounding moments, it looked like the copter would defy gravity and somehow stay aloft despite the smoke and flame pouring from the passenger compartment. Then, it just fell from the sky, crashing into the concrete barricade that separate the highway lanes. The rotors snapped off, flying in all directions as the copter exploded into a ball of fire.

I did not see any way for the pilot and the passengers to survive. I found out later that they became the first of many police officers who would die as Carmella robbed her way to fame and fortune. I often wondered how life would have been different, if I had forsaken the comic code and pushed her out of the van. How much grief and heartache could have be averted?

Cars full of civilians piled up as drivers jammed on their breaks and other cars slammed into them from behind. The closer vehicles, splattered with burning aviation fuel, caught fire, and exploded a few moments after people fled from them.

"That's what I am talking about." Carmella gloated. "That's national news!"

She shut the back doors and climbed over the thugs.

"You're in my seat," she said.

"You're not replacing me yet," I growled.

"Listen, old man," she said icily. "I'm a supervillain, and you're a henchman. You'll sit wherever I tell you to."

Enough was enough. I was about to put her in her place. I mean really let her have it, telling her like it was and how it was going to be, but Franky locked up the brakes and I ate the back of the front seat.

Tasting blood in my mouth, I saw stars around the edge of my vision. Somehow, I was lying on the floor between the driver's and passenger's seats. No one was paying attention to me. They were all looking out the windshield.

Franky kept gasping "Oh, crap! Oh, crap!" over and over again.

I pushed myself up, peered above the dashboard, and looked through the windshield.

"We're done," I said. "There's no escaping now."

Chapter Six

Vortex, the most powerful superhero in the city, blocked our path. Dressed in a tight-fitting, cloud-print body suit, and riding on top of a small whirling tornado, Vortex looked so cool and confident with his perfect hair and pearly smile. He flipped his short blue cape over his shoulder.

A half-dozen hover cameras spun around him, some focused on him, others gathered video of the surrounding area. All of the shots would be combined with computer generated images and built into a three-dimensional, emotion-packed epical that showed the end of SafeCracker's forty year career. With the damage caused by Carmella and the thugs, Joe and I would be walking with canes when we finally got out of prison. We'd traded our retirement for a failed attempt at one more score.

"Well, Carmella, I guess you're right." I could not keep the bitterness out of my voice. "We're going to be in an epical after all."

Next to me, that insane woman, smiled enthusiastically. "We sure are."

In the sky above, a news copter circled us keeping a safe distance away.

Vortex lifted his chiseled chin clearly posing for the cameras. His lean muscles flexed under his cloud-print bodysuit.

"On behalf of the heroes of this city, I, the mighty Vortex, Lord of Wind, accept the challenge of BankJob and SafeCracker."

He cracked his knuckles and smiled confidently.

Franky changed his refrain to, "What do I do? What do I do?"

"You shut up," Carmella snapped.

Joe looked down at me. "Any ideas, Gene?"

I looked up at him. "Let's just surrender."

Joe looked tired. I was tired. Running from the cops and facing down superheroes was once exhilarating. Now it was just exhausting.

"We can post bail and run. Vanish into our retirement," I said. "We can spend our golden years on the beach, drinking margaritas, and soaking up the sun."

"Stay on plan, Joe," Carmella said.

I pressed my point. "Our original teammates will visit. We'll talk about the old days, laugh about the good times, and never think about this job again."

"We can take him," Carmella insisted.

"But it's Vortex." Joe sighed.

"So what?" Carmella sneered. "We planned to face supes."

"Not Vortex," Joe panicked. "He's the best. As tough as they come."

"I got this," Carmella told him as she took her purse from under the seat. She slung the satchel across her body as if arming herself for war. "Let's ice that superscotum."

"I don't think so," Joe said.

Carmella spoke cruelly. "Here's your choice. Stay with your washed-up has-been henchman, and be the big hit at some senior citizens home or come with me to a new era of success and fame. It's him or me."

Lying there on the floor of the van looking up at the both of them, I honestly expected Joe to chose me. A person doesn't just throw away forty years of friendship... forty years of loyalty.

"I'm sorry, Gene."

"It's okay," I said, thinking that he was apologizing for the botched job.

"I want to have a comeback," he said. "I'm not ready to retire. There is so much more to life than growing old and waiting to die."

For a long moment I was confused. I didn't really understand what he was saying to me. Then, as Joe looked to Carmella with a gaze full of hope, I realized the future I'd planned so carefully for so many years was lost. I could not compete with what she offered. Joe always loved the spotlight and she was promising him another go-round of glory. Deep down, I knew he wanted an epical.

"I'm ready to follow your plan," he said. "Tell me what to do."

When jobs went sideways, Joe had always followed my plans. He'd always spoken those words to me, and I usually got us out of the jam. I was the quick thinker. Joe was the charismatic actor. We had always been the perfect duo, a villain and his henchman. Hearing those words spoken to another felt like someone punched me in the stomach. All the air fled from my body, and I just lay there gasping for breath.

She smiled triumphantly, and made a point to stare down at me for a moment, before looking over at Joe and taking charge. "You just walk out there and face Vortex." Her voice purred, sounding silky smooth. "Me and the boys will do the rest."

I grabbed Joe's elbow. "Please don't."

I felt so pitiful. It wasn't about me losing my spot on the team. I was losing my friend. Forty years, all the highs and lows, it was slipping away. She'd planned this whole thing. I knew she did, pushing the situation so Joe would be stuck in the moment, torn between his love of the spotlight and his love for me. No one wants to grow old. Joe saw Carmella as his fountain of youth. I saw Carmella as his death.

Joe pulled his elbow from my grip and got out of the van. By the time I struggled up from the floor, he was already facing Vortex. Carmella was standing by his side, and the thugs spread out in a semi circle flanking them both.

"This is bad," Franky said. "That chick is crazy. Vortex is gonna chew that old man up. You wanna close those doors so we can drive away."

"We're staying." I owed Joe that much.

"Just sayin', stayin' is dumb," Franky said. "We should get away while Vortex is distracted."

"That's not how these things work."

Franky was trembling. "It won't take long for Vortex to kick their asses. Then, he will come for us."

"Teams stay together."

"Hell with that, old man." Franky reached for the ignition.

I blocked his hand, covering the key with my left as I raised my right into a fist. "We don't abandon them."

Franky opened the door and jumped out. "This is a shitty team."

He ran across the highway and climbed the chain link fence. He looked back once before he disappeared into the trash-strewn woods that formed a strip of green between the road and the houses. He'd escape through some person's backyard. He'd probably steal their car and get away, another fine example of today's hired help.

I slid into the driver's seat. Should I go out there and help or stay here just in case SafeCracker managed to get back to the van? I didn't know what to do. For once, I didn't have a plan. The situation was so screwed up that I couldn't see a reason to do anything. If we had surrendered, they would have allowed us bail. They might have even given us a reduced sentence in a low security prison if we promised restitution. Now, the only question I had was how many years hard time would I be serving in federal prison.

Vortex crossed his arms. "What were you thinking? That stunt at the bank was bad form. Bad form indeed. Shooting police officers? All that damage you caused? I am deeply offended at the violence. I am responsible for this city. I..."

BankJob popped a loud chewing gum bubble. "Stop monologuing you ball sack."

Vortex fixed Carmella with an appraising glance. "You're new, so I'll give you some advice. We don't interrupt each other's dialogue. It helps the editors make clean cuts."

"Suck it." She blew another large bubble and popped it with a snap.

Vortex turned back to Joe. "What are you doing, SafeCracker?"

"I'm making a comeback," Joe said. "Just like she said in front of the bank."

"You realize that I have to take a hard line on villains who don't follow the rules. I can't cut you any slack," Vortex said with a sigh. "I'm going to have to arrest you. You crossed the line."

"I understand," Joe said, and started to raise his hands to be cuffed.

"Please, tell your henchmen to lay down those weapons." Vortex said.

Joe turned and opened his mouth to speak, Carmella pulled down his hands and whispered something to him. They argued briefly.

"Is something wrong?" Vortex asked.

Carmella put her fists against her hips and lifted her chin in a striking supers pose. "We're not surrendering."

The hover cameras swirled around her.

Vortex crossed his arms. "Making a fight of it would be unwise."

"Get out of our way." Joe was channeling the confidence of SafeCracker now. In the persona of the character he had played for most of his life, he sounded threating. But I knew him. I heard the doubt in his voice, and the fear.

Vortex shook his head sadly. "Me and the other heroes, we've let you rob banks for the past ten years out of respect for you and your accomplishments. You never caused any damage. You never hurt anyone. We respected that."

Carmella walked forward. "Bullshit. You supes were afraid of SafeCracker!"

Vortex laughed, not in a mean way. He actually seemed a little sad.

"I smell your fear," She made a show of sniffing the air. "LavaStorm and WindRunner quit the scene because they got tired of being outwitted by this man. He's the real deal. Now you're pissing yourself because your producers are making you tangle with him."

"I am here to protect the city I love."

"You're scared!"

"Over my career, I have thwarted six attempts by supervillains to dominate this city. I have fought the mutated minions of DoctorHelix to a standstill. I stood alone against the robots of N.O.M.A.N. last year when the supercomputer tried to gain control of the docks. I am not afraid of SafeCracker." He paused, and then added as an afterthought, "or you, whomever you are."

"My name is BankJob."

Vortex's frown turned into a smirk. "That's quite the name."

"It's going to be a name that strikes fear in superheroes," Carmella said.

"It's not working yet."

Carmella pointed at Vortex and spoke to Joe as if ordering a dog to attack. "Take him SafeCracker."

"Don't do this." Vortex stepped into a fighting stance, still floating on his tornado. "SafeCracker, I came to make this arrest, so some eager young super didn't rough you up. Times are changing. The old code is not followed as much anymore."

"I know."

Vortex nodded, "This new generation of supers don't have to keep things clean enough to be in the prime time news cycle. It's all about the Internet now." He sounded disappointed as if he too missed the old days. "Shocking footage and violence gets more clicks than family friendly content. There's a lot of anger over the damage you caused downtown."

"I am sorry for the damage."

"Let's call it a day before you get hurt. If you surrender, the judge will be more lenient. I'll speak on your behalf. You can say the job went bad. Blame it on an overeager crew. Your reputation should shield you from serious time."

Joe looked back at Carmella. Then he looked at me. Our eyes met through the windshield.

"What the hell is this?" Carmella shouted at Joe. "Stick to my plan."

Joe blinked, and looked back at her. For just a moment, I thought everything was going to be okay. I could almost smell the ocean breeze and taste the margarita on my lips, and then it all faded away.

Carmella waved a finger in Joe's face. "If you want to make your comeback, stay on script. If not, get in the van with that geezer, Gene."

Joe stiffened at the rebuke. He stepped forward and tilted his head back to address the superhero floating above him. "You, Vortex, will be the first of many to fall before BankJob and SafeCracker."

While everyone was looking at SafeCracker, Carmella reached into the satchel she had slung over her shoulder and pulled out a roll of toilet paper and a vial of baby-powder. She tossed them both into the tornado on which Vortex rode. The superhero did not dodge out of the way. Maybe he was over confident and didn't expect an up-jumped henchman to do something overly effective, or maybe he just wasn't worried about bathroom products. I mean it looked like paper and powder. What harm could it do to a super as famous as Vortex?

The wind opened the roll of bathroom tissue pulling the paper out in a long, sinewy tail that grew longer with every revolution in the tornado. The jar of baby-powder didn't have a cap, and as it swirled in the cone, puffy white ribbons of dust trailed out behind the jar. The items spun in the cone of wind swirling upwards toward the superhero who did not take notice until the strip of toilet paper began to wrap around his legs. He moved, attempting to free himself, but the bathroom supplies continued to wrap him.

The dust caused him to cough. The length of paper started wrapping around his waist. He tried to push the paper down, but the cyclone spun the roll around him pinning his left arm to his ribs. His right hand tried to grab the roll, but the growing powder cloud swirling upwards obscured it. The white powder washed over Vortex, engulfing his chest, and finally, his head disappeared in the cloud.

I was too stunned to speak. Carmella laughed loudly.

The wind funnel supporting the city's greatest hero slowed, pulsed, and then fizzled out. Vortex fell through the cloud of powder to land hard on the ground, gasping for breath, and looking like a cartoon mummy.

The toilet paper did not tear easily, not like normal bathroom tissue. It was some kind of sticky plastic material that wrapped tighter around Vortex as he struggled. He was kicking with his legs and pulling with his right hand trying to untangle himself, all while attempting to reform his wind cloud and coughing like a two-pack-a-day smoker.

The superhero did look a little funny flopping on the ground like a fish out of water with BankJob posturing over him. The camera copter was certainly broadcasting live. All the hover cameras were getting the action from every angle. The great Vortex looked the fool. I felt bad for him. His sales were going to go down, way down, and Carmella was on the rise.

I realized that she must have planned this whole thing hoping for Vortex to show up. The violence to lure him out. The specialized gadgets to make him look silly. Carmella knew exactly what she was doing. I had been a blind, old fool. Too busy dreaming about retirement, I hadn't seen any of this coming.

"Get him boys," Carmella ordered, and the thugs leaped onto Vortex.

Our hired goons were punching, kicking, and stomping down on the superhero, laughing and mocking him. Now, I felt really bad for him. This was going to wreck his carefully cultivated image. Internationally known supers don't get beat up by unnamed thugs. This was breaking the rules. Henchmen were the extras. Their purpose was to support the supers. Sure, a henchman worked for their villain, but if the hero threw a good punch, the henchman needed to overreact to the hit. It made the hero look better, which made their villain look better when he got away. Everyone was part of the show. That's what made comics great, heroes and villains striving against each other, but also working together according to a set of unspoken rules. This new generation just didn't get it.

"Okay. That's enough," I said, more to myself than to anyone as I was still watching the spectacle through the windshield of the van.

When the beat-down did not stop, I grew concerned. Two of the thugs were holding Vortex up so the others could pummel him. Why wasn't Joe stopping this? He was just standing quiet, with a shocked expression on his face. Where was my boss of forty years who was always in control of the situation?"

"That's enough," I said, stepping out of the van.

I didn't really expect the thugs to listen, but I expected Joe to take the cue. He didn't even look at me. He just kept staring at the goons who were now clearly in the process of beating Vortex to death.

Chapter Seven

"Stop hitting him," I shouted as I ran over to the one-sided melee.

Carmella watched my approach with a wry smile. Joe's face had a pained expression that I couldn't quite read.

"Stop it, stop it." I tried to pull one of the goons off Vortex. Despite my years of working out, I could not move him. He shrugged me off and went back to pummeling the hero. Our hired thugs weren't rednecks full of false bravado. These thugs were capable of holding their own against heroes.

Twenty years ago, I could have licked the bunch of them. Now I was powerless in the face of their size and youth. Damn them. Were they going to kill Vortex? That was a line I would not cross. Heroes and villains did not kill each other. Villains got arrested and did their time. Heroes sometimes got beat up, but there were never any lasting injuries. Didn't Carmella understand that if villains and heroes crippled or killed each other, the story would be over? For this whole industry to work, everyone had to keep away from deadly violence.

Villains did seemingly dastardly things. They lashed a hero to a train track with a locomotive bearing down or tied a hero to a conveyor belt heading toward a heavy machine press or a giant sawmill blade, but the goal wasn't to kill the hero. Everyone wanted to create the dramatic tension that pulled in the fans. Most times the danger was more hype than actual. The villain always made sure there was time for the hero to wriggle free or be rescued by some other super starting a new crossover series.

To me, superheroes were celebrities. They were characters to be admired and emulated. The best of them inspired people to goodness and gallantry. Seeing Vortex set upon by a bunch of goons, pummeled down to the ground, broke my heart, and I could see it affecting Joe in a similar way. He was yelling at the thugs on the other side of the pile, trying to pull them off.

"BankJob," Joe yelled at Carmella. "Help me stop this."

"Oh, Joe." She acted as if she was bored.

"I don't support this behavior."

"We're just acting for the camera. Putting on a show."

"You're killing him."

"Think of the ratings!" she cried.

"Stop this now." Joe rarely got angry, but he was furious now.

"Don't be a killjoy."

"Stop them, or we are done."

"Okay, okay," Carmella relented. "Boys. I think our twirly bird has had enough."

The thugs stood in a ring around Vortex, rubbing their bloody knuckles and smiling in a self-satisfied way. These young thugs had truly enjoyed stomping the super. What was this world coming to? Where was the comic code? Back in my day, henchmen would never act this way. At that moment, I so wanted to retire.

I rushed over to Vortex and helped him into a sitting position.

Joe clasped Vortex on the forearm. "I'm so sorry."

Vortex blinked with confusion. He was punch drunk. His face was smeared with powder. Toilet paper hung on his limbs. He looked ridiculous. I tried to pull some of it off. The paper wasn't paper. It was feather light strips of Kevlar. Vortex moaned. They'd knocked out one of his white teeth.

Carmella bent down, picked up the tooth, and held it up between her thumb and index finger. One of the hover cameras zoomed in for a close up. She leaned down and smacked Vortex on the temples trying to bring his addled brain into focus.

"Prettier than a pearl," she said. "Thanks for giving it to me, lover boy. I'll have it set in a pretty ring."

One of the thugs stepped forward. "You want me to knock a few more out? You could make a set of earrings."

She thought for a moment. "I'd rather have a necklace. Boys do me a solid and..."

"No," I shouted, ready to fight my own team.

"I think a necklace would suit me."

"That's not going to happen." Joe took the tooth from Carmella's outstretched hand. She looked like she was about to object, but Joe shook his head. She'd gone too far, and she knew it. In his heart, Joe was a good guy. He played by the rules.

SafeCracker knelt down to Vortex. He put the tooth in the hero's palm and closed the hand over it. "You'll be okay. The ambulance is coming. Sorry about this. You know kids these days."

Vortex probably didn't know much of anything at that moment, but he'd figure it out in a few days. SafeCracker and I were old timers, and we lived by the old rules established by the publishing companies that forced heroes and villains to follow strict codes of conduct. Violence was limited and the stories had to be suitable for children.

Vortex was the next generation of heroes, those who came after Joe and I. They were emboldened by Hollywood money. The world wasn't so black and white for them. They could get away with more violence and other things, but they still had rules. They still served the story and tried to honor the code when they could.

Kids like Carmella, and those supers like her, were different. Her kind didn't even try to follow the rules. They embraced gratuitous violence. Worse, they crapped all over the code. These kids didn't just beat each other, they tried to ruin each other. Sometimes they even crippled or killed each other. I didn't understand it, but I knew if this was the industry's new direction, I really needed to get out.

BankJob snapped her finger, "Let's roll, boys."

We piled back in the van. The coward, Franky was still missing in action, so I hopped in the driver's seat and drove past Vortex who was still sitting on the asphalt staring at the broken tooth in his open palm.

I was sick to my stomach as I drove away. Vortex was an honorable hero and didn't deserve to be laid so low. The thugs were all laughing, slapping each other on the back, and giving each other fist bumps. I listened to them regale each other with descriptions of how they punched and kicked Vortex. Two of them got into a fracas over who knocked out the tooth. Carmella pushed them apart laughing as she did. This was what I had to work with. I missed the old team. I missed the old ways.

I blamed the change in attitude on the digital print revolution and the Internet. In the good old days of film, big publishing houses and large movie studios were the only ones with the ability to bring national attention to a super. Because of ease of producing digital media, independent publishing houses and movie studios sprang up pushing aside the old guard. The Internet allowed easy advertising through social media. Soon everyone was trying to out do everyone else in an effort to go viral and hit the big time.

Opportunities were everywhere, competition was fierce, and it was easy for these new heroes to go too far in trying to one-up each other. Why couldn't these kids realize they were going to destroy the industry? The whole business existed on the goodwill of the people who enjoyed the stories.

If this new generation of supers kept pushing things, public opinion would become hostile. Cops, who at one time didn't want to put their kids' favorite villain in jail, would stop looking the other way. Judges who gave light sentences would hit supervillains with maximum penalties. Politicians up for reelection would pass anti-supers laws to appease an angry public. The whole business of being a supervillain would collapse without the support of the people.

Joe was sitting quietly. Was he thinking the same thing?

Carmella reached over the seat back and started rubbing his shoulder.

"You were so cool," she purred.

"We went too far," Joe said.

"No way. Shock and awe. Flash and flare. We had to make an entrance," she said with a wild glint in her eyes. "People needed to notice us."

"I think we broke every window on the boulevard," Joe said.

"And that's great." Carmella purred as she kneaded his shoulders. "You did great."

Joe covered her hands with his own, stopping their movement. "It wasn't right to have everyone gang up on Vortex."

"Oh Joey." Carmella leaned over the seat and kissed him on the cheek. "We'll be more careful next time."

"Promise?" Joe asked.

"Cross my heart." She ran her finger slowly over her right breast. "You can spank me if I break my promise." She laughed lightly. "You know, Joe. I ain't a minion anymore. This opens up a whole new world of possibility."

I gripped the wheel tightly and focused on holding my temper in check.

"Beating Vortex was so cool," one of the thug announced. "I love seeing supers get thrashed. But I think I love doing it even more."

They all agreed

"Hey boss." The thug was talking to Carmella, not Joe. "Did you really take down Vortex with baby powder and toilet tissue?"

Carmella turned to the back of the van. "You know, boys, a girl can't give up all her secrets."

"It wasn't normal stuff," another thug insisted. "I know it wasn't, cause normal toilet paper don't wrap someone up. And it tears real easy. This stuff was strong. Felt strange when I touched it."

"Come on, boss," the thug asked. "Let us in on the secret."

"Since I like you all so much, I'll share," Carmella spoke in a low voice. "They were specially made compounds. One interacted with the energies that Vortex used to fly. The other disoriented him for a moment."

"Where did you get them?"

"I made them."

"Really?" the thug asked. "You must be very smart."

Carmella patted his leg. "I sure am."

I didn't believe her. "How did you really get those compounds?"

"I made them," she said indignantly.

"No, you didn't." I let my doubt show in my voice.

"I am a real super," she said. "I got an A in chemistry. One of the few classes I ever passed. I can mix chemical compounds that do things. Weird things."

Joe nodded excitedly. "She's got compounds in her utility belt to deal with all the local heroes."

It hurt me to see Joe acting like such a tool. I'd seen her little laboratory. The one that Joe paid for. I thought nothing of it. Kids these days created drugs out of cold medicine. I built model airplanes when I was a kid. Everyone had their hobbies.

"I thought you were making bathtub meth," I said.

She laughed. "I was doing that too."

Joe leaned forward. "Carmella's plan is to use trickery to take down the heroes that come against us."

"That's what I used to do," I reminded him.

"I know."

"And it didn't always work," I said. "We spent time in the slammer. I don't want to spend my retirement locked up."

"I've got lots of tricks." Carmella smiled mischievously in that way arrogant young people did when they thought they knew everything.

"And if your tricks fall short?"

"I'll figure it out on the fly. I'm not stuck in a plan. I'm not you, Gene."

Before I could respond to her little dig, one of the thugs in the back seat asked, "We gonna beat up more supers?"

"No." I said loudly. "Absolutely not."

"Actually," Carmella made a show of stretching out the word. "We may have to deal with a few more superheroes before the rest learn not to mess with us. Are you boys up to the task?"

I waited for them all to agree, then repeated myself in the clear authoritative tone that I'd used for forty years. "We're not going to fight superheroes."

They settled down immediately.

"Since when did you become a boss?" Carmella spoke into the silence.

I held the wheel tightly, channeling my anger into the grip and keeping my voice calm. "If you can put on a costume, claim to be a supervillain, and shoot up the boulevard, then I am permitted, no required, to intercede. This team will not break things. We won't harm civilians, and we are certainly not going to beat up supers. Tell them,

Joe."

"Gene is correct,"Joe said, supporting me. "We can't go looking for trouble. And we all need to be on the same plan. No more last-minute changes."

Carmella crossed her arms. "What if they attack us?"

"That's different," Joe said.

She frowned.

I smiled.

"Your comeback is going to be big news," Carmella said, smugly. "We're going to build a fantastic team. I've got it all planned out."

She was confident. I'll give her that. And I knew she was going to use SafeCracker's comeback to launch her own career. Carmella only cared about her success. That's what this was all about. She was a gold-digging little trollop who would drag down our excellent reputation for some fast cash and fleeting fame. I forced myself to keep silent as we drove to where we'd dump the van.

Chapter Eight

I pulled the van into the abandoned warehouse and parked next to the pair of SUVs. I always had one of the thugs steal a commercial van the night before the job and then we transfered to clean vehicles before heading back to the hideout.

Carmella jumped out before I'd even turned off the ignition. She all was hype and attitude.

"That was great!" She shouted, fist pumping the air, and then spinning across the concrete floor like a ballerina.

The thugs piled out leaving Joe and I sitting alone in the van.

"This heist violated the code," I said. "Carmella's actions were against everything we stand for."

He pulled off his mask. I could see he wanted to say something but couldn't find the words. Instead, he chewed his lip looking tired and old, not at all like the man I'd known these past forty years.

Carmella slapped the hood. "The loot is loaded. Time to go!"

I drove the SUV with the money. Joe sat in the passenger seat and Carmella sat behind us but leaned forward. All of the thugs drove behind us in the other vehicle.

"We did good," Carmella announced.

I rose to the bait. "You almost killed Vortex."

"And that would have been a bad thing? He's a rich, entitled jerk that flies around like his shit don't stink. He got what he deserved."

"There is a code to this business..."

"Not any more," she interrupted. "The code was created by a privileged class of people who seek to maintain their authority over the industry. My generation seeks freedom from the establishment. We don't want your limitations. We won't inherit your prejudices. Your hatreds. The new world's gonna be a better place. Time for you to adapt or move aside, old man."

Joe just stared ahead, looking out the window, watching the world go past. I let her have the last word. How could I dispute something I didn't even understand? I knew one thing though, if she was right, then everything I believed was wrong.

We drove to our hideout in silence. It was one of the longest drives of my life. The phone was already ringing when we walked inside the home I'd shared with Joe for the past forty years. Carmella shouldered past me and picked up the receiver. I should be the one handling the calls. As the head henchman, I ran the business end of things.

Sadly, I really didn't have the desire to pick up the phone. The violence against Vortex sickened me. I couldn't shake the image of his broken tooth and his punch drunk face all battered and swollen. He was the greatest hero of the city, and a gang of bruisers without powers had laid him low.

"Carmella," Joe said. "Maybe Gene should take those calls."

If looks could kill, Joe would be a corpse. But my friend held his ground. "Give Gene the phone."

She put the phone on mute, but kept it to her ear. "You want an epical or retirement."

Joe was torn. I could see the anguish in his face. He looked at me, pleading.

"Let her handle the call," I said.

With a triumphant grin, Carmella took the phone off mute and spoke to the caller in a condescending tone that grated on my nerves.

"You better offer more than that if you want rights to our story."
Carmella waited, then cursed some more. "We're not signing any
exclusive agreements, you butt munch!"

"Is she really going to get you an epical with language like that?" I
asked.

"It's a different world," Joe replied.

"It's not a world I want to be part of."

"What are you saying?"

"I'm going to retire."

Joe shook his head. "I need the both of you."

"I won't work with her," I said.

Joe frowned. "We can work things out with Carmella. She's got lots
of plans."

"You can only have one head henchman on a team."

"I know. That's why her coming out as a supervillain is so perfect."
Joe said. "You'll still be my right hand, and she'll be our ally."

"That won't work." I said.

"Don't be that way," Joe said. "You'll like her. The three of us will
go far together."

"She's going to ruin you." I said, harshly. "There is no way a
person like that can be successful."

He opened his mouth to argue, but Carmella put the phone on
mute and asked, "Is five million per epical enough for you boys?"

The thugs cheered. Joe looked tired but happier than I'd seen him
in years.

"See." He said to me. "She knows how to talk to these new
independent publishing houses."

"Congratulations."

"I'm going to get my own epical. Imagine, people watching
my story, feeling my emotions, connecting to me in ways that were

impossible with comics and normal video."

The thugs were popping open bottles of craft beers that I never heard of. Back in the day, we drank Budweiser, Coors, and when times were bad, Busch. The kids were drinking bottles with labels that read Dread Doom and Lily White.

I walked into my room and started packing my things. Everything fit into one large gym bag, even my pictures and mementos. I paused for a moment to look at a photo of the old gang. Good times.

Joe entered the room. He was holding Carmella's epical player. "This is what it's all about. This is the future."

He tried to give me the square tablet-like device with its dangling head pads, but I wouldn't take it.

"Just try this, and you'll see the reason why we can't retire."

"Goodbye, Joe." I extended my hand.

He stared at me, confused. "You're really leaving."

"It's her or me." I withdrew my hand.

"This is our comeback."

"No," I said softly. "This is your comeback and my retirement."

"Gene, you can't leave now. Carmella's caper has us back in the big times."

"It's not worth it." I kept picturing the violence on the boulevard. "Some of those police officers might be dead. How many spectators were cut by falling glass? Look what she did to Vortex."

Joe sighed. "Carmella will keep the violence under control. Today was just an introduction. We needed a big showing. On the next missions, we will tone things down and then jack it up again. It's all about walking the line, working the audience. Carmella has it all planned out."

"Our thugs were going to kill Vortex."

"No," Joe shook his head. "The boys were just making a point.

They stopped when I told them too."

I didn't point out that they actually stopped when Carmella told them too. He just couldn't see it.

"Joe, the heroes are going to come for you. You know that, right? Carmella's challenge. Stomping Vortex. That's going to backfire."

"And what if it doesn't. What if we can keep beating the heroes?"

"Those heroes are two decades younger than us. The heroes we outwitted back in our hey-day are all retired. We should be retiring!"

"Carmella says my experience gives us an edge. I'm going to explore my computer controlling powers. There is a lot more automation these days. It's not just turning tumbles in bank vaults. I can get corporate jobs. My power gives me control over security robots..."

"You're missing the point," I said.

He talked over me. "And Carmella's got some tricks of her own. We beat Vortex and he was the best in the city. We can beat the rest of them. It will be like old times again. You and me outwitting more powerful supers."

"With Carmella?"

"Yes. We need her. She understands this new generation."

I looked him right in the eye. "There is no place for me on this team."

"Don't be that way."

I could see he was getting angry, but I was beyond angry. Joe had made his choice in the van, the only thing left for me to do was gather my things, and drag my broken heart from the hideout.

"What way?" I asked.

"Jealous that Carmella did what you couldn't do anymore."

I took a deep breath. "I thought I was doing what we wanted. What you and I wanted. A house on the beach. Some time together without the job and the pressure."

"That's what you wanted." Joe had the good grace to look a little sheepish. "You feel old. I don't. I'm not ready to give up the life. Carmella says a villain with my experience should be able to run rings around these youngsters. Let's give it a try."

For a brief moment, I considered it. Could I put up with Carmella just to be with him? Everyone wants to think they can be young forever, but then a healthy dose of reality settled in. Truth was, I didn't enjoy high-speed chases anymore. It was a lot of work to plan a bank job. My back hurt. My knees hurt. My eyes were going. I just wanted to rest.

"Honestly, Joe," I said. "I was looking forward to retirement."

"I need you, Gene." Joe grabbed my arm. "Please stay. You can help keep us on the right track."

"I don't think I could."

He pointed to Carmella who was talking on two phones at once. "She's got great ideas. She's got great energy. But you have a sense of things. A grounding that's always kept us safe."

"I followed the unspoken rules. I held to the comic code. We didn't hurt anyone. We didn't damage stuff. We made the heroes look good, and they cut us the slack we needed to build our fan base.

"Carmella's trying to compete with the heroes. That's wrong. It's not a competition. It's cooperation. Heroes and villains need each other. We are two sides of the same story. It's okay to outwit the heroes, but you can't do what she just did. There's rules to the game, and she's breaking them in a way that won't end well."

Joe didn't reply. He just looked over at Carmella who was holding the landline receiver up in the air while shouting into her cell phone. "You might be my attorney, but I'm going to cut your balls off if you screw this up."

She raised the cell above her head, lowered the landline, and shouted into the receiver. "You're damned right there is a new supervillain in town, and her name is BankJob. She's teamed up with SafeCracker, and no bank in this city is safe."

"Look at her go," he said. "Do you remember when we had that kind of energy?"

"I do. And we had great times. We took in big scores over the years. But I'm tired. It's time for me to be done."

He sighed. "I think I want one more score. Something big so the world will remember SafeCracker."

"The fans will always remember you, Joe," I said. "You're a classic villain from the golden age."

"I'd like some new fans. Carmella's right. I need an epical to cement my legacy."

I didn't know what else to say, so I just told him the truth. "Carmella's just using you."

"No. She's not."

"She is."

"Maybe, but then we're using each other."

"You're the established villain. She's attaching herself to you so she can use your name to get noticed. You're a stepping stone. Nothing more. She'll leave you in the end."

"Of course she will," he said. "But in the meantime, I'll have my comeback. She'll get established. We'll be helping each other. You'll see."

What I saw was an impending train wreck. There was no way I could hold this runaway train of a situation on the right track. I needed to get off at the station. "I can't be your top henchman if I don't believe in the plan."

"Give it time."

"No."

Joe looked more hurt than angry. It was settling in that I was not going to stay. "Why not?"

It was hard to explain, but I tried. "We had friendship. We had respect for the law and ourselves. We had an understanding with other supers."

"That's not how it is these days."

"And that's why I'm done. The industry is moving in a different direction. I don't want to work with people like Carmella and our current crop of thugs."

"You can help me teach them the way it should be."

"They don't want what we had."

"How can they not?" He looked genuinely confused.

If he didn't understand, I could not explain it to him. "Goodbye, my friend."

"Fine," he said and turned away.

As I was leaving, I heard Carmella screaming into the receiver, "Are you shitting me? You're wasting my time! Don't call until you can offer me more than six figures on the movie deal."

Chapter Nine

I got my house on the beach, the one Joe and I had planned to purchase together. I filled the shed with surfboards and purchased the '68 Mustang convertible Joe and I had always talked about buying. The solitude suited me well. My only visitor was the meter reader each month, and she just gave a friendly wave. No conversation was okay with me. When the sun shined, I enjoyed the beach. When the rain came, I watched the clouds and listened to the thunder roll.

SafeCracker got his epical, The Adventures of SafeCracker and BankJob. I think I could have come up with a better title, but I was not consulted. Joe and I were done. Forty years of friendship lost. He didn't talk to any of the old crowd, and everyone despised him for it. They boldly promised to boycott his epicals. One even took to social media to set the record straight.

I was not so vindictive. Truth be told, I was eager to see his story. Any connection to my old friend was better than no connection at all. I missed him, but I didn't miss the life of crime. I longed for the little things we did together, like making meals or folding laundry, our day to day life in the hideout. I'd give anything to play a board game with him, to roll some dice, and laugh around the table. Those were the moments of memory that caused my heart to ache.

With the wireless head pads stuck to my temples, I turned on my brand new epical player. I closed my eyes, and the story jacked into my head. The Adventures of SafeCracker and BankJob did not disappoint.

Energy flowed from the head pads into my brain, showing the images, giving sound and touch while stimulating my emotions. The epical overwhelmed my senses. Now, I understood how people became epic junkies.

Epical #1 recounted the activity at the First Union Bank. The events had been substantially changed, dramatized to make Joe and Carmella larger than life. She had been totally sensationalized, her real personality stripped away to create this new tough-girl villain forced to crime by circumstance.

In the bank, she didn't try to pull the ring off an old lady's finger or encourage the muscle to brutalize the helpless hostages. Instead, all that was blamed on me, Gene, the dim-witted head henchman with a perchance for violence against the weak.

The revised events blamed me for the standoff with the police. I delayed everything by having a meltdown outside of the bank because I didn't want a girl on the team. I have to admit the re-telling seemed so life-like that I began to wonder if maybe I was a sexist jerk.

I stopped second-guessing myself when the epical showed me encouraging the violence against the police and Carmella as the one who objected. With subtle editing, a few voice overs, and some computer generated graphics, my character had been totally re-written.

This change to reality hurt like hell. How could Joe consent to my character assassination? At least, he could have asked them to use a different name. Or maybe, that was how Joe remembered the scene. That thought was an icy fist squeezing my heart.

Numbly, I continued watching. In an over-hyped, slow-motion scene, Carmella made her spontaneous transformation into BankJob, pulling off her henchman outfit and declaring herself a supervillain. She singlehandedly led the team out of the bank, fighting desperately through a torrent of bullets.

Though Carmella's overt sensationalism turned my stomach, I kept on watching through the chase scene and where a computer generated voice pretending to be me demanded Carmella commit the violent acts.

Predictably, the defeat of Vortex, had been modified. BankJob's take-down of the superhero looked fantastic. They must have used real footage from the news camera interwoven with computer generated images. The fight was classic super-stuff, done real-well and old school. I loved it, despite Carmella's role in it.

Then, my scene persona ordered the henchman to beat-up Vortex. No mention of knocked out teeth was made, because that would have made Vortex look too weak. I guess his super identity was still valuable property.

Through the brutal beating, the epical pushed emotions into me. I felt terrible for the downed super, but when Carmella ordered them stop beating him, the manufactured emotions of the player clashed with the real-life anger I felt at the change.

I wanted to jack out, but like a moth drawn to a flame I stayed to watch the end. Back at the hideout, the angry caricature of me adamantly argued that a girl couldn't help lead the team. Some of the words were mine, but much had been subtly changed. As I listened to my computer generated voice berating the Carmella the epical forced me to feel sorry for her. I raged inside, fighting the manufactured emotions with real feelings.

The scene wrapped up. SafeCracker fired me, and BankJob concluded the episode with a monologue about progress, equality, and getting with the times. The sentiments were truly beautiful, and she delivered them so well. I would have been inspired, if I didn't know the manipulative monster behind the mask.

Every member of the old team called to express their outrage at my characterization. I told them it didn't matter, but it did. The betrayal had broken a part of me. On good days, I hit the beach. On bad days, I just wandered the house. Funny thing was, I still watched the show because I loved to watch Joe.

In Epical #2, Joe got a new head henchman. A thick-boned Russian dude in his late forties with a square jaw, broken nose, and buzz cut. His name was Boris, and he claimed to have worked security for DoctorHelix. He had a thick accent, and couldn't handle concepts more involved than kicking down a door or busting someone's face.

In the episode, the team robbed another bank. They took too long gathering the money or maybe Carmella purposely lagged. The police arrived, a firefight ensued, and the team was trapped in the bank. Two of the henchman got killed by SWAT snipers, and everything looked done for the team. Then, Franky flew in with a stolen emergency copter. He'd driven to the local hospital and held the pilot at gunpoint forcing him to fly the rescue mission. The team got away.

In Epical #3, Joe finally got to try his powers in a corporate espionage mission. SafeCracker and Bank Job got hired by a shady arms broker to infiltrate the headquarters of Mektron Industries to steal plans for a prototype super computer.

Carmella planned a smash and grab mission. Shock and awe would carry the day. They crashed through the front doors in a new custom van. The henchmen burst out, blazing away with assault rifles.

The epical made the scene seem so real. I could jump from perspective to perspective seeing and feeling the action through the eyes of the characters. Or I could walk through the scene totally immersed in the action with bullets flying past and feeling the concussive force of the explosions. I smelled the gunpowder. Epicals are intoxicating.

The human guards fled before the onslaught, and I got to feel their fear through the player. I felt the excitement of the thugs as they blazed away causing needless damage. I didn't access SafeCracker's emotions or BankJob's. I just watched in third person view as he circumvented the security system so she could recover the computer core.

The trouble started on the way out. They were attacked by security robots. Powerful machines that gunned down the henchmen, blasting through their bullet proof vests with lasers.

SafeCracker and BankJob had a long running fight through the corridors pursued by the robots. My heart was beating like a jackhammer when BankJob was knocked unconscious by a concussive blast and the last henchman was killed in a fusillade of laser beams as Boris held him by the elbows and used him as a human shield.

The machines seemed to attack with an inhuman viciousness. They had no mercy. One of the machines closed in on SafeCracker. It had buzz saws for hands and clearly intended to chop up my friend. The epical player enhanced my fear. I trembled on the edge of my seat.

Joe had always been able to control mechanical things. That's the heart of his power. He opened tumblers by commanding them, and as that robot closed in on him, he shouted, "Stop!" The machine paused. SafeCracker focused his mental energy on the robot brain and somehow gained control of the machine. He commanded the robot to attack the other bots and in the chaos of the battle, he escaped with Boris who carried BankJob over his shoulder as if she was a sack.

The epical caught the full emotion of the scene. When watching from Joe's point of view I really felt his desperation and his sudden wonderment at being able to control the robot. In Carmella's point of view I felt her rebellion against an oppressive world that she believed kept her down. The emotions conveyed by the epical were so powerful that I almost accepted she was a hero fighting for the common good. I had to shrug off the effects, because epicals only showed emotions that fit the narrative. Just like video, radio, and print before, epicals only tell the story that sells.

Epical #3 put them on the fast track to incredible success. Some criticized Boris for using the thug as a shield, but others raved at his resourcefulnesses. The narrowness of their escape truly made for great entertainment. Everyone was talking about the new dynamic duo and their butt-kicking head henchman Boris.

Joe had his fame. He was bigger now than he was in our heyday. I could not have done this for him. With BankJob at his side, he transcended his generation. He became a dashing older gentleman making a comeback by embracing new ideas and technology.

SafeCracker and BankJob were an unstoppable team, grabbing the cash, outwitting the police, and defeating a local hero in every episode. The ways they beat the heroes were absolutely genius. Carmella would design something special for each, and by using a combination of chemical compounds, mechanical gadgets, and plain old-fashioned trickery, she made them all look like chumps. None of the heroes saw it coming. The fans loved it. I was impressed.

Maybe Joe deserved this glory in the twilight of his life. Even as part of me felt lonely and lost, another part of me was happy because Joe looked happy. I always wanted the best for him, which is probably what made me such a good head henchman, and dammit, I was a good leader. We had a great run with lots of good times, and we never hurt anyone or stole anything that wasn't insured by the government.

The show fell into a familiar pattern, following the same format for each episode. Joe and Carmella would decide on a mission. Carmella did the planning, because Boris proved to be dumb as a stump. He kept the minions in line using a heavy hand, but was useless for anything that didn't involve violence.

Carmella certainly knew how to ramp up excitement. To prepare for Epical #4, she announced that they would be robbing a bank. She announced the name of the bank and exact time the robbery would occur. She encouraged the bank president to hire the best security possible.

On the date, a half dozen supers surrounded the bank, along with police and hired security. BankJob had tossed down the gauntlet and the super community had risen to the occasion.

BankJob fooled them all. She drove a tunneling machine up through the floor of the bank to avoid the defenders who were all waiting on the streets outside. SafeCracker opened the vault, and they were in and out before the authorities realized the money had been taken. It was one of the only episodes that wasn't filled with violence, but later it came out that BankJob wanted to blow up the bank and Joe wouldn't let her. The building had been constructed in the 1800s and was a historic landmark. Joe had always appreciated old-time architecture.

For the next few episodes, BankJob continued to announce the bank that would be robbed, and the duo used some kind of technology to outwit the defenders. Everything was videoed by the hover cameras that accompanied them. Their emotions during the mission were captured by implants and then combined with the video. It was all so exciting.

Carmella was a master at circumventing the powers of a superhero. As the episodes continued, it became clear that the robberies were of secondary importance. Carmella liked beating the supers, and the audience loved her for it. After the mission, there would be a little heartfelt review.

The technology they used in the jobs was expensive, and I worried about Joe's finances. Some of the devices were probably rented at a discount from genius inventors trying to market their products, but still the cost would have to be staggering. I couldn't see how the scores alone could cover the cost of the jobs. I worried Carmella was running the team in the red, hoping to generate future profits from entertainment contracts and licensing agreements. I also worried about the increasing amounts of devastation BankJob left in her wake. The violence appalled me. She and her goons shattered windows, exploded cars, and wounded police officers. In Epical #6, Carmella blew up a person's home just to create a diversion. The fans seemed to love the plan, but I thought about the lifetime of mementos that must have burned in the flames.

The violence toward the supers who tried to arrest them increased with every episode. As "The Adventures of SafeCracker and BankJob" grew in popularity, the damage to the heroes increased. The writers tried to blame the violence on the mental trauma Carmella sustained while working as a henchman under the violent, dim-witted Gene, but it was hard to hide her credulity.

Epical #7 centered on the efforts of StarStreak and Phantomena to arrest the team. This was a crossover episode, involving the publishers of all three supers. The media made a big deal of the build-up. StarStreak and Phantomena gave tons of interviews promising to end the violent crime spree. Both heroes ended up in the hospital after BankJob lured them into a warehouse and then exploded the structure.

The media justified BankJob's actions by characterizing her as a desperate victim. According to them, she was the darling poster child of a new generation struggling to give voice to their oppression, but I didn't fall for it. I knew Carmella. I knew the business and understood how the producers were trying to balance reality with the hype necessary to create an anti-hero star in these modern times.

The scene where StarStreak said he didn't have any hard feelings nearly turned my stomach. I wondered how much he got paid to express that false sentiment. Phantomena refused the interview, and I had to give her credit for not caving to the pressure. I heard later that she lost her contract because of it.

By Epical #8, the story became more about BankJob and less about SafeCracker. BankJob planned the heists. BankJob negotiated with the geniuses to get the tech. BankJob beat the heroes and became the central character. An over-sexualized, hair-flowing montage celebrated every successful heist. I had to take off one of the head pads because even with the emotion filter turned down, I was starting to like Carmella. The experts who say that epicals don't mess with a person's perspective are flat out lying.

Their first blockbuster movie came out around the same time as Epical #10. The movie's title was "BankJob" with no mention of SafeCracker who ended up being a minor character. The movie was biographical in nature, highlighting how Carmella Cosine transcended her lowly middle class roots to hit the big time. With many scenes of social ostracism by rich kids during her school years and much parental abuse by an overbearing, hard-drinking father, the movie became a smashing success with the younger crowd.

"BankJob" showed Carmella joining SafeCracker's crew and suffering as a henchman under the dim-witted Gene. The movie concluded with the emergence of BankJob who was shown as the embodiment of victim empowerment. Her attack on the police and her defeat of Vortex became a heroic stand against authority.

Everyone had their opinion on why the movie became so popular. Some critics praised the producers for showing BankJob as a good person forced to do bad things by nature of the system. Of course, I knew Carmella was just an evil, self-centered tramp trying to get rich, but the show gave her aspects of a crusader. The producers knew that so long as she seemed to be fighting for a cause, the audience would grant her some latitude. The movie walked that line better than any I'd ever seen before.

One commentator, praised BankJob's attack on privilege, calling her a self-made super. The girl started as a poor, abused minion, then transcended her lowly position to become one of the most famous supervillains in the nation. Because of the hype, most people didn't mind if a few big-time, ultra-rich supers got hurt by an underprivileged young woman trying to get ahead in a world stacked against her.

BankJob also resonated with the disillusioned demographic of people who felt that world had wronged them somehow. Most in this group objected to authority. Many viewed the government as oppressive. They naturally distrusted the police, and praised BankJob for her violence against them.

I heard later about some Internet sites where miscreants kept a body count, awarding extra points when BankJob caused a particularly nasty injury to a police officer or security guard. This horrified me, and made me realize that Carmella was right in one observation. I didn't understand these new fans at all. They were not the kind of people I wanted to entertain.

Ultimately, I believe the reason why BankJob got so big in that first year was because most people want to disclaim responsibility for their actions. Everyone who does bad things wants to believe they are a good person deep down. Carmella portrayed BankJob as someone trying to be better. Her rise to fame is a fine example of the extent that a person can avoid culpability for their misdeeds because of situations that negatively impacted their life.

Of course, BankJob's carefully crafted image could not last forever. Sooner or later the true Carmella would shine through all the glitter and glitz. I didn't have long to wait.

Chapter Ten

Three weeks after the movie premier, I was laying on the beach enjoying the sun when a shadow fell over me. I opened my eyes, and immediately concluded that I'd fallen asleep and was in the middle of a crazy dream. Joe stood over me.

I knew something was wrong, really wrong. He wasn't wearing his SafeCracker suit. Heroes and villains always wore their costumes whenever they went out in public. The hover cameras wouldn't follow a super who was out of costume. Every appearance was a chance to be in the public eye, a chance to be newsworthy and gain renown.

"I know it has been more than a year," Joe began. "I'm sorry about that. I'm sorry about everything. I just wanted to come by and tell you that…" He paused for a moment, overcome by emotion. "And I also wanted you to know. You were right about Carmella. Right about everything. I should have listened. I should have retired, but I just wanted one more score."

I knew from the tone of his voice that this was no dream. Maybe a nightmare, but not a dream. Joe turned away. I tried to call after him, but my voice caught in my throat. He walked like an old man, his shoulders slumped and head down. Beaten. Broken. He almost looked like he needed a cane. I finally finding my voice.

"Joe," I called to him.

He paused for just a moment, a slight hesitation as he lifted his foot. I thought he might turn around, but he didn't. I heard the sirens far in the distance, police cars wailing to somewhere. His pace quickened. He was walking to my gate, leaving me lying in the chair.

"Joe," I called again. "Wait."

He kept walking. I ran after him, moving to block his way. I wasn't letting him pass until I got some answers. "What's wrong?" I almost added, "Boss." Habits established over forty years were hard to break.

"I'm turning myself in," he said, cocking an ear to listen to the sirens.

The wails grew louder. The police cars were headed this way.

"For what?"

Joe looked confused. "You haven't heard?"

I stared at him.

Tears formed in the corners of his eyes. "I killed them." His voice cracked in a strangled sob. "Two little girls… a boy…and their mother. I killed the whole family."

"You?" I asked, not believing it. "Tell me what happened."

"It was a car chase. Five police cruisers… Franky crazy-driving the van through mid-afternoon traffic... Carmella wanted to bump up ratings with a big escape scene. We were right on schedule. The bridge was going to open. Franky would jump the river, and we'd be free." He blinked, causing a tear to fall. "Dammit, Gene, Carmella just wanted to look cool for the camera. She didn't need to do it."

"Do what?" I asked.

"Carmella says to me, 'time to bump up the ratings' and she climbs to the back of the van where she opens the rear doors. I tell her, 'Be careful not to lose a money bag.' What a jerk I was."

He scrubbed a tear from his cheek. Joe had always been a tough man, hard as stone, and to see his misty eyes made my heart ache for him.

"I was worried about the money! The damn money!" He took a

breath, trying to master the anger he felt at himself. "Well… Carmella steps out onto the back bumper, barely balancing. She's got one hand holding the loading strap hanging down from the van's roof. Using the other, she picks up this giant machine gun. It's much too heavy for her. She's laughing as she pulls the trigger. Bullets spray everywhere. The cop cars veer off."

Joe paused, struggling to speak the rest of the story. The wailing sirens grew louder, and my friend seemed to realize he was running out of time. He drew a deep breath, and finished his story in a weak monotone voice that weighed on my heart.

"One stray bullet hits a young mother. She's with her three children. They're driving home from an ice cream parlor. The bullet only grazed her arm and totally missed the kids, but she lost control, and drove off the side of the bridge. Everyone was tightly seat-belted in. The whole family died. Three little kids… and their mother."

Far down my street, the first police car turned the corner. A half-dozen hover cameras whirled around the vehicle. This was going to be big news. Two more cars followed the first. A news vans turned the corner. They were ready to get the story.

Tires screeched as the police cars stopped in front of my house. The sirens went silent, replaced by the sounds of shouting officers. A hover camera flew over the top of my wooden fence. It's lens focused on us.

Someone pounded on my front door.

Joe reached out, squeezing my arm in a gesture of friendship. "Goodbye, Gene. Please tell the others that I'm sorry I lost touch with the old team. Tell them… tell them the years together were the best of my life."

Two more hover cameras flew over the fence and circled around us. They would record the final arrest of SafeCracker. At least, I'd be by his side. I opened the gate, and as we stepped through, the cops saw us. They pulled their pistols, crouching low in defensive firing stances.

"He's not armed," I shouted, holding Joe back. "He called to surrender himself. Please, don't shoot."

"He deserves a bullet," snarled a cop who aimed a law enforcement assault rifle and looked eager to shoot. "Him and that bitch put enough of our friends in the hospital."

"I don't deserve a quick death," Joe shouted, stepping past me. "I deserve to suffer." He shrugged off my arm and walked towards the officers. "Shoot me if you want. Or lock me up. I want your retribution."

I could not run after him. Any quick movements on my part might start the officers shooting. It was clear they wanted to kill him. Being a cop was rough these days. The men and women in blue had paid the price for BankJob's high ratings.

Sheltering behind the wooden fence, I watch Joe stagger toward the officers, who did lower their guns. They must have felt pretty silly pointing firearms at a shaky old man with tears flowing down his cheeks.

A black van screeched around the corner, and raced down the street so erratically that I knew Franky must be driving. A dozen hover cameras kept pace with the vehicle. BankJob was coming, and I felt a flash of terror that sent a shiver down my spine. What terrible thing would she do?

BankJob's van came to a halt behind the line of police cruisers. Franky parked right next to the news trucks. The front passenger's door opened and BankJob flounced out, "Are you ready to party?"

The side door slid open and Boris jumped out with a big pistol in his hand. He was followed by a half-dozen henchman in body armor. They cradled machine guns in their steroid-pumped arms and opened fire immediately, totally outclassing the cops. Police car windows shattered in explosions of glass. The air hissed from deflating tires.

The cops fled, all but one brave trooper. The officer with the assault rifle stayed in place, shielded somewhat by the front of a cruiser as bullets ricocheted all around him. It was clear to me that he didn't want to run in the face of BankJob's lawlessness. He held his ground, firing at the thugs as they walked toward him. The rounds bounced off their heavy body armor. One of the brutes tossed a firebomb onto the cruiser he was sheltering behind.

The officer ran as the car exploded. He sprinted down the road, clearly intending to reach the other cops who were hiding behind the wall of the neighbor's house. He never made it. Boris lifted his pistol, took careful aim, and shot the office in the back of the head just before he reached safety.

As the officer died, everything seemed to grow so quiet. Boris put his pistol away, and stood there looking smug as if daring anyone to protest. The cops had all taken cover. No one else was going to mess with the team.

The hover camera spun around. Dozens of bystanders had their phones held up. Everyone was waiting to see what happened next, except me. I just wanted this whole horrible moment to end.

BankJob sauntered toward Joe. "Where is your costume?"

"I'm done," Joe told her.

"You ain't done," she circled him like a predator toying with prey.

"I'm tired," he said. "I'm so damn tired."

"We have a contract with our publisher. Twelve more epicals. Season 2."

The hover camera circled them. I didn't want this scene in the next epical.

"Let's go inside," I interrupted, then added in a whisper. "People don't need to see Joe like this."

"You ain't on the team anymore," Carmella said. "And besides, all publicity is good publicity. Ain't that right?" She shouted to the newscasters. "Show them the good and the bad. We've got nothing to hide."

"I just can't do this anymore," Joe said, pitifully. "Let me surrender to the cops."

She shook an index finger. "No. No. No. You break that contract, and I lose millions. The Adventures of SafeCracker and BankJob will finish the run. Then, old man, you can do whatever you want."

Joe shook his head.

"You're gonna finish the contract."

Joe straightened up in defiance, looking just a little like the Joe I knew. "I'm done."

This was my cue. I stepped up to my friend's side. "If Joe says he's out, then he's free to leave."

"You think so, old man?" She asked.

"It's a fact." I said, like I would have spoken twenty years ago in the prime of my youth.

Carmella gave a little laugh, then looked over her shoulder, back to the van. "Boris?"

"I'm here, boss."

"This is Gene," Carmella said, lazily pointing to me. "He used to have your job.:

"Yeah, boss."

"Could you shoot him between the eyes?"

"Sure thing, boss." He seemed to think real hard and then asked, "You want me to do it now? Or should I wait 'till like you say so?"

"Let's see what SafeCracker wants," Carmella suggested. "So Joe, here's the deal. You come with me and fulfill your contract, or I have

Boris terminate your friend. What's it going to be?"

"Don't hurt him." Joe slumped in defeat. "I'll keep doing it."

Carmella flashed me a triumphant smile. "Gene will enjoy his retirement as long as my checks keep coming in. You understand?"

He nodded, and she took him by the arm.

"Wait a minute," I said. "I can take care of myself."

Joe hesitated. I could see he didn't want to go.

She tugged on his arm and he followed.

I ran after them. "Stop."

I grabbed her arm. She looked at me like I was a bug, then easily pulled free of my grip. Her lazy backhand struck my cheek and stars burst over my vision. I toppled to the ground, and before I could rise, Boris loomed over me, waving his pistol in my face. "Touch her again, and I'll ventilate you."

I could only watch as Carmella pushed Joe into the back seat of the van.

"It will be okay, Gene," he shouted. "It's only one year. I won't extend my contract. Not for all the money or the fame in the world."

Joe tried to say more, but one of the thugs shoved him to the back as they all piled in. He struggled against them, but they were twice his size and forty years younger.

Boris still looming over me gave me a parting kick to my ribs that rolled me over onto my back.

"You have a good day," he sneered.

I wanted to say something witty, but I couldn't find my breath. That kick from Boris had really hurt. I was having trouble breathing. My old body couldn't take the hits like it once did.

Boris walked to the van, swinging his shoulders like he'd just won a championship boxing match against a top contender. He slammed the side door shut so I could no longer see my friend struggling against the minions in the back seat.

Franky started the engine, which came to life with a puff of black smoke. Carmella blew me a kiss as she drove away. I closed my eyes, trying to block out the pain. It wasn't only my side that hurt. The thought of Joe, trapped in the back seat, broke my heart.

A short while later, the sergeant knelt down next to me. "You need an ambulance?"

"No," I said, sitting up.

"Sorry we pointed the guns at you and SafeCracker," he said. "I grew up reading his comics. We didn't understand what made him change."

"He didn't change!" I said. "He's a good man. Those comics showed the real SafeCracker! Don't believe those epicals."

The sergeant patted my arm. "We didn't know how things were. Now we do."

The confrontation at my house exploded onto social media. I had to hire private security to keep people away. Everyone wanted to know the real truth, and I wondered how long the carefully constructed public image of BankJob would hold up under the scrutiny.

Chapter Eleven

The death of an innocent is something every supervillain fears. Heroes and villains both try to minimize injuries to bystanders because hurting your fans is a sure way to turn the crowd against you. When accidents do happen, supers pay big money to the injured party or to their families in cases of death.

Joe expressed terrible remorse. When he spoke on talk shows, he did so with tears in his eyes. His pain was genuine. He gave a huge settlement to the family.

BankJob did not shed a tear. She blamed the police for not breaking off the chase and heroes for not saving the family. She criticized the government for forcing people to wear seat belts and the car companies for installing them. Social media exploded in anger when her lawyers were able to get the charges against her and SafeCracker dismissed on a legal technicality.

Epical #13 showed the heist where the mother and her three children had been killed. It was a heart-breaking episode that included the scene at my house. The writers didn't pull any punches. The epical showed SafeCracker as remorseful and revealed Carmella as cold and calculating. I thought everyone would hate her, but many of her fans stayed loyal. They criticized the mother's driving skills. They characterized the distraught father as a greedy parasite trying to benefit from his family's death. The media spun the controversy and everyone profited except the victims.

SafeCracker and BankJob continued pulling heists through the next few epicals. Brazen daylight smash and grabs that blasted holes in bank walls and left a trail of beaten supers and injured police officers. I figured the producers were just trying to maximize the profits. I didn't think that anyone in the show cared about the longterm.

The news was full of rumors. I could not keep up with them all. The hired thugs were on late night TV giving exposés of the team, alleging copious amounts of drinking, drugs, and sex. All the lurid tales of wanton wickedness that work to raise short term profits. BankJob denied all of these claims with her characteristically colorful language, alleging they were all blankety-blank, money-grubbers looking for a media handout.

One of the rent-a-thugs, a skinny chap named Lapinski, said candidly on one talk show, "I had to quit the team because I couldn't stand to see that poor old man brutalized by that evil bitch. She runs the team like a tyrant."

BankJob's response was typical of BankJob. "SafeCracker and I are a dynamic duo. We're a perfect team. He's got the experience, and I got the sex appeal. BankJob and SafeCracker forever!"

When the reporters asked about the allegations made by the thug, she explained them away. "I fired that blue-balled loser for being a cowardly shit stain. Don't believe his trash talkin' retaliation."

The talk show hosts never got the chance to ask Lapinski any follow-up questions. He was found a few days later with a broken neck. After that, the rent-a-thugs got the message and stopped giving interviews, but the questions kept being asked.

The police investigation of Lapinski's murder turned up some evidence linking Boris to the crime, but the evidence was mysteriously stolen from the evidence room at police headquarters.

BankJob was like a star going supernova. Anyone could see the house of cards was falling down. A book publisher sued for the return of their advance. Victims sued for restitution. Even die-hard BankJob fans who professed to love "her gutsy style" and "her real-world profanity" concluded that maybe she had gone too far.

By Epical #19, the media was calling BankJob and SafeCracker criminals. I cried like a baby when I first heard people saying it because I knew how much the moniker must have hurt Joe. The difference between being classified as a villain and a criminal was huge.

Being called a supervillain gave status. A villain made lots of money, and police often looked the other way. When a villain got caught, the prosecution made sweet deals, and if there was a trial it was just a publicity sham, and the judges always gave easy sentences.

But when a villain goes too far, they are treated worse than a common criminal. Everyone has the opportunity to bring them in or put them down. Super criminals didn't enjoy the protections of the industry.

Over the next couple of epicals, it became sickeningly obvious that the producers were building up to a climactic showdown. Carmella became more erratic. Joe was despondent, almost unable to act. The last few episodes focused on Carmella and her loud-mouthed minions talking trash. Joe only had a few appearances at key points. I became acutely aware that the producers didn't care if SafeCracker or BankJob survived.

The last episode of the series, Epical #23, was a double-sized bestseller that chronicled the death of SafeCracker and BankJob. It had three different collectible cover images and cost three times as much as a normal epical, but everyone bought it, even me. We just had to experience the details of how the story ended.

On their last heist, SafeCracker and BankJob never even made it into the bank. The authorities had finally had enough. The police hid inside the bank, and Vortex, StarStreak, Phantomena, and a dozen other local superheroes waited on the roof to help the police catch the criminals.

When Franky pulled up in front of the bank and everyone piled out, the police just opened fire with armor piercing rounds, execution style. The thugs were gunned down in a hail of police lead. Franky got one in the head, as he tried to drive away, but Boris pulled up a manhole cover. He used it like a shield, then as the superheroes charged in, he dropped the cover and jumped down into the sewer to make good his escape.

Dodging the bullets, BankJob and SafeCracker fled on foot to the next intersection where BankJob flagged down a sporty convertible. The driver was all smiles until BankJob punched him in the head. She dragged him out of the car, and punched him repeatedly until he collapsed on the ground.

It looked like SafeCracker didn't want to accompany her, but she forced him into the passenger seat.

"Stay there or I'll kill him," she shouted.

Joe just hung his head, looking so tired and beaten.

BankJob slid over the hood to the driver's side. She stomped on the vehicle's owner one more time before speeding away.

In previous epicals, the writers would have included manufactured content to justify BankJob's treatment of the driver. He would have seemed a scummy lawyer or callous businessman and deserved the stomping because he used his privileged to take advantage of others. That's how epicals manipulated a person's perspective and made villains into heroes.

In this case though, the epical made the viewer feel sorry for the driver. He was characterized as a father of three who provided for his children. The epical didn't give all the details, just enough content to pull at the emotions and let the viewer justify the reasons for their anger against SafeCracker and BankJob.

From the overhead views, the high-speed chase looked like a snake sliding through the streets. The superheroes driving their eclectic mish-mash of super vehicles formed the body. The dozens of police cruisers racing behind looked like a long twisting tail. Carmella, the head, always seemed to know just where to go, missing all the roadblocks and traffic jams.

The red-haired femme fatale drove even crazier than Franky. She escaped the city, blew through the suburbs, and headed up into the mountain roads with a pack of supers on her tail. Vortex was in the lead, zooming along on his speeding tornado. Right behind him, zipping along like a ray of light, was StarStreak. The rest of the supers came after, driving a motley collection of super vehicles that reflected their personalities. I didn't recognize most of the supers in the chase.

A few times, it looked like Carmella might get away on those twisting mountain roads, but as she drew close to the peak, it looked to me like she was getting desperate. Her smooth movements became jerky. Was Carmella getting tired, or was it some kind of trick? The car's gas tank must be getting close to empty. I knew she'd need to do something soon. Then, as she came to the mountaintop, she poured on the speed. I figured she was trying to break away. Maybe she knew a dirt road switchback, or a cave, or some other way for them to escape. Turns out she was only thinking of herself.

The epical showed the end in horrific detail, but my mind kept replaying the image as it was shown on the evening news. A hover camera caught it all, following right behind the convertible, giving a first-person view of the end. I could hear the engine's rise and fall as BankJob shifted to an even higher gear. Her hair was blowing wildly. She was laughing. SafeCracker was desperately holding on. He looked old and tired and so very sad, bracing himself but knowing the end had come.

The turn on the mountain road was much too tight, and the car was speeding much too fast. Honestly, it didn't even look like BankJob was trying to make the turn. The front bumper smashed through the flimsy wooden railing sending splinters everywhere. The car launched out into the sunset sky, rising higher and higher and passing in front of the red, swollen sun. It seemed to be soaring toward the twilight clouds. For a moment, I really thought they were flying. Did the car have some kind of anti-gravity field? Would a jet engine thrust from the trunk? Would wings sprout from the fenders? Did BankJob have some secret get-away planned? She was always so resourceful.

Its momentum spent, the car reached the pinnacle of its arc. The camera copter closed in quickly on the car getting a good shot of BankJob and SafeCracker in the front seat at the apex of their ride. The front dipped down, and the trunk came up. BankJob gripped the steering wheel, laughing maniacally. Joe just stared ahead as if resigned to his fate.

BankJob separated from the car, pushing up from her seat. The convertible fell from the frame as the news crew in the copter focused their camera on BankJob. She was holding onto a backpack which she pulled over her shoulders and belted around her hips. A pair of rockets flared to life, and she zoomed off into the twilight sky.

My stomach fell out from under me as if I were in the car with Joe. The pilot brought the copter around, just in time for the camera operator to refocus on the plummeting vehicle and get the money shot. The car impacted on the ground and then exploded into a ball of fire. My friend did not deserve to die like that.

I checked the news every couple of minutes, hoping that the supes had caught that wicked woman, but BankJob had made a clean getaway. No one had expected a rocket pack, and the only pursuing supers who could fly were Vortex and StarStreak, and they didn't chase her. They left after the crash, and everyone said they were scared of taking on BankJob. This made sense to most people because she had promised to kill them the next time they tangled. It surprised me though because I had admired Vortex and StarStreak. They, like Phantomena and a few others, continued the tradition of courageous caped crusaders.

I could not accept how much the world was changing. I smashed the epical player. It was a wasteful thing to do, but I didn't want to ever see those images again. I didn't want to remember SafeCracker that way.

My heart ached as I retrieved the old SafeCracker comics from their place on my bookshelf. Tears flowed down my cheeks as I read from the yellowed pages. Forty years ago, in the flower of our youth, we had been everything we could dream and this was how I wanted to remember my friend.

The lawyer visited me two days after the wreck. Joe and I had prepared our wills together twenty years ago. We named each other as the other's sole beneficiary, so I was going to get all of Joe Hannock's estate. There was, of course, nothing left. Everything he'd worked for was gone.

The lawyer explained, "Against my advice, my client, Mr. Hannock, withdrew large chunks of his invested capital. He used his retirement funds to finance his comeback. It was clear to me that the woman was influencing him, but there was little I could do. It was his money. How could I stop him?"

It all made sense now. Carmella wasn't just after Joe's reputation. She was after his money.

The lawyer continued, "The only thing left is a small life insurance payout, approximately 10,000 dollars. It's a burial policy, but since the car exploded and the fire burned the body to ash, the estate will incur no funeral expenses. I have the check here for you."

I waved it away. "Donate the money to a victim's fund. That's what Joe would have done."

The lawyer gave his final apologies and departed.

Chapter Twelve

Four days later, a monsoon hit the coast. It was the kind of storm that shook the world. I listened to the ocean roar and the wind howl and wondered if the water would rise and wash me away.

Late that night, in the midst of the torrential rain, the doorbell rang. I expected to see a police officer demanding that I evacuate, but I opened the door to find Joe standing in the porch light, soaking wet.

"Hello, Gene," he said, his voice shaking. "I know I have no right to come here. And I'm not here for any handouts. I just have to tell you something. Can I do that? Please."

I couldn't move. I couldn't speak. Was this a ghost or some horrible prank?

He continued speaking. "You don't owe me anything. I treated you terribly. I know I burned the bridges between us. I understand why you hate me. But just listen. Please."

Was this really Joe? Was my friend alive? I had to reach out and touch the door jamb for support. My knees trembled.

"I just wanted you to know that you were always the most important thing in my life. Our friendship meant everything to me. Your advice and your planning were always dependable. I'm sorry for treating you the way I did. I'm sorry I destroyed our friendship. I was a fool. The blame is totally mine. I ruined it. I ruined it all. For this, I'm so deeply sorry."

He turned away and was halfway down the walk before I could

speak.

"Joe," I called. He turned back to look at me.

I ran out into the rain, water soaking my slippers, rain pelting my face. I threw my arms around him, hugging him in the wind. "It's really you. You're alive."

"You can hate me," he said. "You should hate me. I hate myself."

My chest tightened at the empty tone of his voice, my poor friend. I could not hate him. I would not let forty years of friendship be erased by what had happened. Joe needed me, and I needed him. I pulled him under the porch overhang. "Don't blame yourself."

We stood facing each other, dripping wet, but out of the rain.

"I can't come in," he said. "I've said what I came to say, and now I have to go."

"Go where?" I asked him.

"Where all evil people belong... jail... the cemetery."

"You're not evil."

"Evil is as evil does," he whispered.

Eager to change the subject, I asked, "How did you survive?"

"Alright, I'll tell you the story. Then, I'm leaving. Agreed?"

"Just tell me."

Resigned, he began his tale. "BankJob drove us off the cliff. Just like you saw. She turned to me, laughing and said, 'It's been a fun ride pops, but it's time for me to move along.' Then she unbuckled and flew away."

He sighed. "The convertible started falling. The copter flew past. I watched the ground grow closer. I knew I was going to die, and I was glad... glad that it would finally be over.

"I just kept thinking what a fool I'd been. She used me, my money, and my workshop. I'd let her ruin the legend of SafeCracker that you and I had labored a lifetime to build. I didn't want to live with that shame.

"My fiery death could set things right. The villain who became a criminal would get what he deserved, and be a lesson to others who would choose my path. I was dropping through the air, listening to the wind rush past, knowing the only real regret I had in life was how badly I'd treated you."

He took a deep breath. I could see he was struggling to hold back tears.

"How did you survive?" I prompted.

"The news copter and all the hover cameras sped off after BankJob. A bunch of young heroes were trying to take her down. Not one camera had stayed on me, so no one saw the rescue.

"Vortex landed on the convertible. He ripped off my seatbelt and plucked me right out of the falling car. The operator in the news copter did turn at the last moment so the epical would have the impact of the car and the explosion."

"Everyone assumed I was still in the vehicle, because Vortex had zoomed us into a cloud. We flew for a time, then he descended into some trees. We landed in a small clearing. All the town's big-name heroes were there. All the ones Carmella and I had made fools of over the past two years. No reporters. No paparazzi. Just a bunch of sour-looking heroes.

"I figured I was in for one nasty beating. We'd really hurt poor StarStreak, scarring his handsome face. Phantomena still walked with a limp. Vortex had lost his tooth. Everyone there owed me real payback.

"I was ready, but all of them just stood around me in a circle, staring down. I didn't feel like fighting. I wasn't threatening them. Actually, I wanted the beating.

"Gene, I hoped they would kill me slowly for all the horrible things that I'd done in my comeback crime spree. I wouldn't have argued. A quick, fiery death was too good for me. I deserved a slow, painful end."

Joe fell silent.

"What happened?"

"It was an intervention. Vortex and the others told me they admired the honorable way that I had conducted my business over the years. They respected me for the villain I had been before I met Carmella. Then, they told me that Carmella was a gold digging little tramp that had used me. I told them that I'd known. I'd seen the truth by epical six or seven, but by then I'd spent all my money financing her gadgets so I could make my comeback."

"They asked me why I didn't leave," He paused and ran a hand through his wet grey hair. He wouldn't meet my eye.

"Why didn't you leave?"

He looked at me. Then, he looked away, ashamed. "I tried to leave before that family got killed. I really did. By Epical #9, I couldn't take it anymore. I told her so, and she became furious. I was afraid. Carmella threatened me. She said splitting would hurt her image, so I was stuck until she was established. I figured it would only be a few more months."

He covered his face with his hands and pressed his palms against his forehead. "Then that family died, I just had to get away. That's when I came to you and tried to turn myself in," Joe struggled to hold in a choking sob. "It was hell after that. She slapped me around. She called me names. Threatened me."

"You should have left." I said, feeling his anguish. "You could have come to me. We would have figured it out."

Joe didn't say anything.

"You could have come to me," I insisted.

He shook his head. "I stayed with her for the last year, because she threatened your life. She would have sent the goons to murder you. I couldn't even kill myself, because if I did, she said she would take it out on you."

His face was red with emotion, his eyes wet with tears. "When our car went off the cliff, and I saw the ground rushing up, I thought, 'Thank God. It's all going to be over.' Of course, it's not, not yet anyway."

"You escaped the supers?" I asked.

He gave a bitter laugh. "No. They let me go. Vortex told me they'd heard how I was coerced. They felt sorry for me. They let me go on my promise that I'd never pull another job. I told them to take me to jail. Vortex said in that haughty way of his, 'No court could punish you more than you are punishing yourself.' StarStreak patted me on the shoulder and said, 'We really respect you. You're the victim here.' Then, they all walked off, leaving me so ashamed."

"Joe, none of this is your fault."

"I let BankJob onto the team. I let her push you out. It's all my fault. I betrayed our friendship, our principles. All because I didn't want to get old and become a has-been. All I had was the business and my image. If I wasn't SafeCracker who would I be?"

I was starting to feel a little guilty too. Carmella had come into our lives like a force of nature, beautiful and ugly, both at the same time. It was easy for me to see what she wanted, but not so easy for Joe. Her beauty had blinded him. I'd only seen the ugly.

"It's not all your fault," I said. "I am responsible too. I abandoned you."

"I forced you to leave," he insisted. "I was blinded by her charms. I bought into her dream. I wanted to be in the spotlight again. I wanted to feel young one more time."

This recrimination was going nowhere. "Joe, at this point blame is irrelevant."

"You're probably right." He started to turn away.

"What are you doing?"

"It's time for me to go."

"Go? To where?"

"It doesn't matter."

"It matters to me."

I laid my hand on his arm. "There is no need for you to leave."

"I have to."

"Come inside. We'll have a drink, some food, and talk about tomorrow."

"Just like old times."

"Just like, but without the robberies and car chases."

"It'll never be the same between us."

I realized Joe was crying. Not some sobbing breakdown, that wasn't his way. He was a strong man, even now with everything gone wrong. I could see the tears slipping from the corners of his eyes, but he still held his dignity. He'd come to tell me I was right and to say he was sorry. He'd done that, and now, he fully intended to go off to suffer his fate. Without money or friends, he'd die on some street, a lost soul with nothing and no one.

I held his shoulders and looked him in the eyes. He wasn't leaving my porch. "Stay."

"How can you forgive me for what I did when I can't forgive myself?"

"Just stay."

"You must hate me."

"I don't."

"You should."

"Come inside."

"I have nothing to offer," he said. "I'm an old used up crook. The world has changed, passed me by, and left me broke and broken. I don't know why Vortex saved me from the crash."

"He saved you because you're a good man."

Joe made to leave again, and I grabbed his arm with all my strength. He winced under the grip. "Stay!"

"I won't be a burden to you."

"Joe. I need your help on a mission, and I can't do it alone."

"What mission?" he asked.

"Retirement. You and me at the beach, sipping margaritas. Me learning to surf. You tinkering with your machines."

His laugh was bitter as he motioned to the house around us. "You don't need me on that mission. You've done great."

"The beach has been our plan for a decade. This was the house we picked out. The car in the garage is the one you wanted. There's even an empty room for your workshop."

"You knew I'd come back?"

"I hoped you'd come home."

"I don't deserve your friendship."

"My plan for retirement requires two people. You and me. Don't make me spend these years alone." The thought of life without him just hurt too much.

"You'll just let me move in?"

"In a heartbeat."

"After all I've done, you'll just forgive and forget?"

"There is nothing to forgive," I told him. "You wanted a comeback. I wanted to retire. You walked your path. I walked mine. And here we are, together again. Let's pick up and move forward."

He shock his head. "It can't be that simple."

"But it can be." I hugged him. "You and me together facing the twilight of our lives."

"No." He gently pushed me away. "I don't think I'm ready to retire."

"Not ready?" I gasped. "Not yet!"

The shock and disbelief I felt must have been reflected in my face because he smiled then, giving me that grin that I hadn't seen in years.

"I want to retire with you," he spoke in an earnest voice. "I really do, but I can't. I've got to fix the damage I have caused. Carmella hurt a lot of people, and I didn't stop her. Her sins are my sins, and I have much to atone for."

Then, I understood. Joe wasn't going to just go off and die. He had just come to set things right, and then somehow he was going to get back in the business. "You can't rob banks again!"

"I agree," he said. "SafeCracker died in that car wreck. He's dead to the world and to me. I am going to become someone totally new."

I saw in his eyes, behind the pain and shame, a hint of my old friend. His strength and courage surged up, and I knew then that he would overcome the heartache of these past two years. I knew with a certainty that he would pick up right where he left off, but he would not be a villain.

"You know, Gene, I'm developing a plan, reinventing myself. Opening locks is what I do, but I can affect anything with mechanical parts. It's not just sliding open bolts and spinning tumblers. I can control machines."

I nodded, understanding where he was going.

"When we first started, the world was not automated. Now, there are machines everywhere, and I have the power to command them. I can take over security systems, robots, computers, anything controlled by circuits or automated with mechanics. Now, that's a real super power."

"Sure is," I agreed.

"But it's more than that. I watched Carmella. I learned how she built those gadgets, and it gave me an idea. " His features hardened with a new resolve, and I knew my friend was back. "I'm thinking that if I built a bunch of simple machines and placed them under my control, I could use them like a swarm."

"Yes, you could."

I looked into his eyes, and asked, "What will you do with these machines?"

"I want to go after her. I want to bring BankJob to justice." He took a deep breath. "I know I'm an old man, but I still have some fight in me."

My heart began to beat. I felt its rhythm in my chest. I could not keep the smile off my face when I said, "I'd like to see you put BankJob behind bars."

"Well, you will. I'm going to put her there. Not for money or fame or anything more than it's the right thing to do."

"I'd like to help you."

He offered me a small whimsical smile. "I'm going to need a superhero name."

"You'll think of something."

"I'm going to need a new costume."

"I might be able to help with that," I said.

He reached out and took my hand. "I hoped you would because I want you with me, by my side."

"I'll be there."

The joy in his eyes made my heart hammer. I wanted him to be happy.

"There's one problem, though," he said with grave seriousness. "Hero's don't have henchmen or minions. You're going to have to be my sidekick."

"Your side kick?"

"Yes, and you have to wear a super costume?"

"We'll be partners?" I asked him.

"Absolutely," Joe deadpanned. "And our costumes will have to match."

The laugh we shared together felt so good. Then, arm in arm as life-long friends, we went inside and started sketching costumes and brainstorming our supe names.

Epicals: And Being Super

Around the middle of the twentieth century, scientific advances changed the world. Humans split the atom, developed computers, created robotics, and cracked the genetic code. It was only a matter of time before people started applying this new science to improving the human body, and the first supers came into existence.

At first, the exploits of these extraordinary individuals didn't capture mainstream attention. In fact, the people of that early era lived in a world with different values. They'd suffered two world wars, lived with the threat of nuclear annihilation, and got their news from heavily controlled sources. They didn't embrace the impossible with the same exuberance of modern people.

In the last two decades of the twentieth century, a small group of steadfast supers were fighting crime, saving people, serving governments, and generally making a real difference in the world, but their existence did not become mainstream knowledge. Most comic fans of this time-period assumed everything they read was fiction.

Stories about superheroes and supervillains filled the pages of comic books, but there was no way to separate fact from dramatic invention. People still viewed the idea of costumed characters with super powers as mostly fiction.

Police departments and government agencies did rely on heroes to help them fight the villains, but their involvement was always kept quiet. The governments of the world didn't want the average people knowing about supers.

In the comics, real characters were lost amid imagined characters as each comic publisher created more fantastical stories, but as time passed and the scope of super-science increased, there was less fiction and more fact in these comic books.

Around the turn of the century, a few scientists and inventors developed a theory postulating the existence of underlying forces in nature that explained the universe better than existing science. They identified twenty types of energy that interacted with each other to produce all sorts of impossible-seeming effects. It was a unifying principle that brought together old-world magic with modern technology. Of course, their work was poorly received by the academic community and heavily censored by governments unwilling to allow the public access to super-science.

Everything changed with cell phone cameras and social media. These, coupled with the power of the Internet, changed the dynamics of information supply. Over the next decade, people became indisputably aware of supers' activity. The world governments could no longer hide the possibility of human advancement through super-science. A new industry developed as 'being super' became the next big thing.

People gain super powers in vastly different ways. In the beginning, most supers seemed to acquire their skills accidentally through exposure to unique anomalies in nature or prototype technical processes gone wrong. Freak storms, solar flares, toxic rain, falling into a vat of chemicals, freezing to death, and even extreme heat caused spontaneous mutations giving rise to extraordinary abilities. Science had not yet discovered mystic energy so the development seemed random.

Even today, the process for making a person super is not really understood. Hopefuls can use many technological methods, ranging from genetic modification to the implantation of cybernetic devices.

There are faith-based or magically derived methods. Some supers have even claimed empowerment by alien beings.

While some people, are self-made supers, most have to use a specialist who offers a trans-formative process. Most specialists cling to traditional science or turn to magical ceremonies found in ancient texts. This lends credence to the new unifying theory of mystic energy, which explains why processes based on that body of new knowledge are generally more successful.

The prices for these experimental procedures are very high and success is not guaranteed. In fact, the processes rarely work. Most hopefuls are left unchanged, and sometimes, instead of making a super, the process will cause death or terrible mutation. Nowadays, humanity is divided into three groups.

Normal people still make up most of the population. These are the same old human beings who have walked the earth since ancient times. They go to work or school, pay their bills, and live their everyday lives. They're called "norms," and there's nothing wrong with being normal.

Supers only make up a small percentage of the population. All supers have super abilities. Some can fly, while others can tunnel underground. Other abilities include augmented strength, increased health or stamina, regeneration of injuries, control of temperature, invisibility, transposing through walls, telekineses, and heightened senses. Some supers control machines, while others control beasts. Super skills are as varied as the people who become supers.

The last group are the 'duds'. For every super, there are many duds. These are the people who tried to become super and not only failed, but really bombed it. They don't look human anymore. Duds get all kinds of twisted deformities. Some are worse than others, but most people would rather be dead than a dud. Both norms and supers ostracize them. Many duds choose to live together in slum towns and have become a new underclass. Duds gain super abilities along with their deformities, but the price for their skills is often tragic.

By the year 2020, supers had become big news. Almost every city had their heroes, villains, and duds. The entertainment industry embraced the heroes and villains. People loved them. They could not get enough of them. Book deals, public appearances, movie contracts, and television shows meant money, money, and more money for everyone in the business!

Supers became the new celebrities of the world. Paparazzi followed them everywhere. Scientists, mystics, crackpots, and criminals made big money selling promises of super transformations. The numbers of supers increased and, tragically, so did the number of duds. And then, a new type of entertainment technology was invented which caused an even bigger explosion in the industry.

The epical player was advertised as "television transformed' or "movies magnified to magnificence". The video played three-dimensionally in a person's mind through the use of head pads and included sensory and emotional simulation that made the viewer truly feel like they were a part of the action.

Epicals were just what the norms wanted. Everyone got the experience of being super with none of the risk. Eager fans could put on the headset and live through the serialized missions of their favorite heroes and villains.

Mystic Realms

The Mystic Realms exist as a multiverse of interconnected worlds and parallel time lines. Every possible world and alternate world exists within the cosmos of this reality. Heroic champions wander these worlds. They are proponents of destiny, and their actions can change the course of existence.

The Mystic Realms are united by fundamental energies that flow like rivers of unseen power permeating all things and everyone. People from different places refer to the energies by different names, such as mana, chi, essence, vaki, and 'the force', but they all refer to the same primordial energy that holds the universe together.

Twenty types of mystic energy have been identified in the universe: chaos, chemical, cold, decay, earth, electric, fate, heat, holy, necrotic, order, profane, psionic, radiation, sound, time, toxic, vitalic, water, and wind. Together, these fundamental energies explain every aspect of the universe.

Mystic energy will coalesce together into concentrations of power. The energies are generally invisible, but as concentrations increase or when they are used by people, the energy can sometimes be viewed by the naked eye as swathes of color. Each energy has an associated color.

In the Mystic Realms, magic and science are two sides of the same coin, as both can be used to manipulate the twenty fundamental energies. Everything that can be accomplished with magical ceremony can be wrought through the development of technological procedure. Every realm is linked by consistent natural laws, arcane practices, and scientific principles.

Some realms are places of hope where people struggle to bring their world out of a time of suffering or work cooperatively to maintain an age of order and peace. Other realms are grim places where darkness clouds the land, and the people endure as their world slowly slides into oblivion.

In some realms, magic reigns supreme, and in others, science controls the world. Apocalyptic military conflicts, paranormal events, and terrible natural disasters often give rise to global power shifts. A realm can swing like a pendulum, moving from a state of high magic or astounding technology to a mundane world where both forces have been forgotten.

But in every realm, there are people whose lives resonate through the multiverse. Some are average everyday people with greatness thrust upon them, while others seem to be blessed by the secret designs of destiny. Either way, these champions rise to the challenges before them, struggling through adversity to become a force of destiny in their world.

The Void, the endless space between the realms, is a place of ideals where the patterns of existence form. The physics of a world is created in the Void. Light and Dark. Gravity. The turning of the seasons. The cycle of Life and Death. The concepts of Good and Evil. Every aspect of existence is defined by rules shaped within the Void.

Inside the Void are ageless spirits with eon spanning memories of the many lives they have lived and the many worlds they have walked. These spirits are the core of existence, the heart of magic, and the reason the realms exist.

The ageless, eternal spirits of the Void create the realms by their dreams and fill them with all the wonder they can imagine. Every life lived, every story told originates from the Void. Without the spirits, there would be no life in the realms, no stories to be told. The worlds would be empty, bereft of all purpose, lacking the people that give meaning to the creation.

To leave the Void and enter a realm is the goal of every eternal spirit. When it is time, a portion of the spirit comes from the Void and joins with the growing body to create a person. At the moment of joining, the part of the eternal spirit separates from the Void and does not remember all the other lives it has lived because it is only a fragment of the greater whole.

The new person grows and experiences the world without the benefit of their greater spirit's ageless wisdom. When the spirit returns to the Void, it will see all it has done, the good and the evil, in the fullness of their existence.

The stories of these people, all from different realms, unite in a common thread of magic that moves the multiverse along the spectrum of existence. While worlds rise to greatness and fall into oblivion, the Void will exist eternally for as long as there are spirits who can envision their dreams into existence.

The following entries describe five additional worlds that exist in the infinite universe of Mystic Realms.

Guildhall: Age of Order

The Five Gods came together to create a utopian world. In the Age of Nature, they filled the world with living things. During the Age of Life, peace and prosperity existed for three thousand years, but the realm was torn asunder by greed, prejudice, and fanaticism. The Five Gods were slain, and the world fell into the Age of Death.

After suffering for 1,000 years, a group of heroes arose to drag the world from the ashes. They gathered knowledge and founded an organization they called Guildhall. Its members, called guildsmen, returned peace to the world by establishing a cooperative world government.

For the past 1,000 years, Guildsmen have worked to maintain the world they have built in the Age of Order. Peace is fragile. Prosperity is fleeting. The same feelings that destroyed the Five Gods remain in the world, and the final age, the Age of Chaos looms.

Empire of Tyrs: An End to Hope

Meredia is a grim, dark world of dying dreams and clockwork machines where hope seems an empty promise. Aberrant magics flow tainting the land and transforming people into monsters. Cultists abound, demons sow seeds of destruction, and hordes of undead spontaneously rise. Ghosts haunt lonely ruins, vampyres hunt the night, and vicious beasts prowl the wild lands.

Emperor Tyrs rules the world of Meredia through military force and massive magic-driven machines. Armored airships circle the sky and mechanical behemoths shake the ground. He sits on a golden throne in a city of smoking factories overseeing a diverse world of different peoples and cultures that include elves, klactons, minotaurs, orcs, pythians, and weetles.

The Empire was born of humanity's last hope, but the violent world of Meredia could twist even the noblest of dreams. The emperor promised peace and propensity to all, and the senate vowed to see his dream made a reality, but after the wars ended and peace came, neither had the power to fulfill their intentions.

The might of the Empire is everywhere, but its strength is powerless against the Grim Dark, an energy that taints the land and the people.

Everstars: Life on the Galactic Frontier

An experimental science based on mystic energy, known as genesis cell research, destroyed Earth centuries ago. A few million people escaped annihilation by fleeing on a starship called the Ark, which used a prototype faster than light jump drive to leave the solar system. After becoming trapped in a hyperspace jump column for many years, the Ark emerged into an unknown spiral galaxy the survivors named New Eden.

Humanity began rebuilding their civilization by settling along one of the galactic spirals. They inhabited seven solar systems by terraforming worlds and building space stations. These worlds united into the Galactic Coalition. Though shaken by intersystem wars, the government maintains power. However, social unrest is common. The galaxy is divided into those who have too much and those who don't have enough. Aristocratic families and powerful corporations control most of the wealth.

Society is composed of humans, androids, genetically altered humans, called GenEs, and humans who have been transformed by the warping forces of hyperspace, called Mystics. The New Eden galaxy is a place of extremes where science and mysticism compete to create a culture of starships and sorcery.

The rich live in the seven Prime Systems named after old earth mythological figures and places. These are well-developed worlds with sprawling cities and magnificent space stations. The people living on the Frontier Systems are not so lucky. Settled planets are owned and operated by wealthy individuals or powerful corporations and inhabited by indentured workers and the poverty-stricken unemployed. The Galactic Core is a dangerous place filled with discontents and criminals.

DoomFell: The End of Tomorrow

Some say humanity's greatest achievements occurred in the

decades just before the end of their civilization. In those final years, advances in technology altered the world and the people lived in a time of technological opulence.

Genetically altered crops could feed the world three times over, the sun was harnessed to provide limitless energy, cybernetic enhancements improved the human body, robots replaced the labor force, and engineering improvements allowed domed cities to be built under the sea and in other inhospitable climates to end population pressures. Humanity was on the brink of settling the moon.

The world was at peace, without competition for resources. There was no reason for nations to fight. In this new age, the rich got richer, and the poor got rich. Everyone and everything were moving forward and getting better. Then, suddenly, civilization crumbled. One small systemic failure led to another, and in the cascade of collapse it, became the end of days. Plague, Famine, Death and War! Afterward, a blanket of ash covered the earth, and the peaceful silence was broken only by the infrequent sobs of the few who had lived through the end of tomorrow.

The great cities are jagged towers of steel and stone reaching up to the grey sky. The buildings are battered by screeching winds, acid rains, and radioactive storms. The sprawling suburbs are wastelands of bramble lawns and rotting dreams. The survivors struggle to make a life in this harsh new world fighting against degenerate mutants, reanimated corpses, power-mad dome dwellers, and silica-sentient robots.

About Author

Anton Kukal is an author, actor, and adventurer. After serving in the United States Army as an armor officer, he graduated law school and enjoyed a highly successful legal practice. Then, he decided to embrace his creativity by developing the Mystic Realms multiverse of interconnected worlds and parallel time lines. Anton is now a full time writer. His website is antonkukal.com.

Acknowledgments

Thanks to those who provided inspiration and assistance. Judi and the other authors at the Bogart's Bookstore Writers Club for their support and encouragement. Danielle for suggesting I write a story about a supervillain's henchman. Pat for editing the early drafts. And the many members of the Mystic Realms Community who have helped bring these worlds to life over the past three decades.

Thank you for reading

One More Score

If you enjoyed the book, please leave a review on the platform you used. Reviews make a big difference for the author!